THE ECLIPSE

THE ECLIPSE OF MIND

BY

SWAGATAM SENGUPTA

ISBN 978-93-5458-157-1
© Swagatam Sengupta 2021
Published in India 2021 by Pencil

A brand of

One Point Six Technologies Pvt. Ltd.

123, Building J2, Shram Seva Premises,

Wadala Truck Terminal, Wadala (E)

Mumbai 400037, Maharashtra, INDIA

E connect@thepencilapp.com

W www.thepencilapp.com

AUTHOR BIOGRAPHY

Swagatam Sengupta is a fiction novelist. He has completed his graduation from Kolkata, India, and after his graduation he started his career. Like our all shades of life, his job career has also lots of shades. At the beginning of his career he was in aviation industry, then as a real estate marketing manager and after that in a senior position in Banking industry.

But when he was in fifteen years of age, he started writing. From that period of time he was a drama writer in all India radio and he wrote lots of short dramas based on history of city roads, comedy, horror, mystery and thriller. He was awarded for recitation and story writing. He wrote lots of stories and poems in magazines and newspapers.

His Bengali poetry book **Shabdohin shabdo** (Soundless Sound) and a sentimental love story, based on a relationship of a father and a son, **Rik- a confined little heart** has been published internationally. His crime thriller **The Chastisement** is also published worldwide. He believes that his life has so many colors and every colors carry a different story. So, writing is his passion, he doesn't bother that how much he will earn and how his book become a best seller. He thinks that when your life will convert into the ink on the paper, then definitely this story will be interesting.

CONTENTS

ABOUT THE AUTHOR..06

ABOUT THE AUTHOR

Swagatam Sengupta is a fiction novelist. He has completed his graduation from Kolkata, India, and after his graduation he started his career. Like our all shades of life, his job career has also lots of shades. At the beginning of his career he was in aviation industry, then as a real estate marketing manager and after that in a senior position in Banking industry.

But when he was in fifteen years of age, he started writing. From that period of time he was a drama writer in all India radio and he wrote lots of short dramas based on history of city roads, comedy, horror, mystery and thriller. He was awarded for recitation and story writing. He wrote lots of stories and poems in magazines and newspapers.

His Bengali poetry book **Shabdohin shabdo** (Soundless Sound) and a sentimental love story, based on a relationship of a father and a son, **Rik- a confined little heart** has been published internationally. His crime thriller **The Chastisement** is also published worldwide. He believes that his life has so many colors and every colors carry a different story. So, writing is his passion, he doesn't bother that how much he will earn and how his book become a best seller. He thinks that when your life will convert into the ink on the paper, then definitely this story will be interesting.

1.

Green desert all around. The fun of returning home after a long time is different. This road does not seem to end. He was lying on the back of the jeep He closed his eyes and thought about his full family, about his wife and children, although he had told her once before on the phone that she was coming this afternoon, he had repeatedly told her not to let his daughter know by mistake, that he did not want to lose the joy in her eyes when he saw her suddenly. Greenery on both sides, the sun almost setting, and for a while. A strange cold frost seemed to make his body intoxicated. This is a strange happiness, a strange feeling that may not be understood by anyone else.

On May 3rd, 1999, he received a sudden call. This Indian soldier had to arrive in Cargill, on emergency duty. It was his naughty sweet girl's birthday. This time she was 5 years old. But it is no longer a birthday celebration He had to carry the bag on his shoulder and go out to defend the country. He looked at the five-year-old girl and her mother with tears in her eyes. He said goodbye with a stone on his chest, I don't know if we will meet again. He made this promise before he waved goodbye, come back once, then celebrate birthday, decorate the house again, maybe. The country is sleeping peacefully because of the promise they have made to protect the country.

On July 26, 1999, the war ended, but he could not return home. He had to go on an unknown and another duty.

Today he is returning home after almost a year and a half of fighting. A strange joy in his mind, a reckless joy of getting to his people brought him the dream of a new day. This time a long vacation, he thought he would go somewhere far away with his daughter, and his wife, Darjeeling for seven days after that marriage, he has not gone anywhere since then. An army jeep took him to the front of his house His home environment is very beautiful, quite far from the city. A bungalow surrounded by a beautiful garden, and a huge pond inside, sitting there on vacation was his biggest hobby. The scent of green and beautiful flowers all around made him forget the smell of poisonous gunpowder. He got down from the jeep and picked up the bag on his shoulder.

When he came to the house, he was surprised, so much crowd in front of his house? He realized that his heart had been pounding with excitement for so long that he had suddenly changed his language. An unknown fear engulfed him in a few moments. He slowly entered his house, crossed a garden and then his house, he saw all his neighbors lined up around him, their faces filled with sadness, looking at him with a dumb look. He couldn't hold himself for long, dropping the bag off his shoulder and running towards the door. He entered the house and saw a large crowd. He even asked a neighbor what had happened, and everyone was standing in his room, but all the unanswered answers made him even more upset. When he entered the house and pushed all the crowd, he never dreamed of what he saw. Two bodies covered with white clothes; the two blood-stained faces are asleep forever. She broke down in tears and came to them. He asked everyone like crazy, when did it happen, how did it happen? But then everyone was speechless. No one came to put his hand on his back to offer any consolation. The pain that came out of his chest was the only question that kept coming back to him in the form of tears, why did he do it and who else did it. How the whole life changed in an instant.

2.

The launch was shaking violently due to the storm, and Rudra had a high fever and severe headaches. He was resting inside, actually sleeping with medicine. He did not know how long he had slept. He got off the train and took the launch, then about three hours journey, he heard it, so he did not waste time.He would take a little rest in the inner room of the launcher with the medicine to fix when he did not understand the eyes. Rudra Sen, an ex-commandant officer of the Indian Army, is currently an agent of Defense Intelligence. Age 36, height 5 feet 10 inches, skin color pale but light tan. Information from Defense Intelligence about the sick body he came to in this remote wilderness. George Stanley's Mental Hospital, established in 1942. Here all the defense mentally ill armies are treated those who are criminals in one way or another in defense, this center is for the psychiatric treatment of those who have been declared mentally ill by the Defense Court. In the middle of the deep jungle and river, this George Stanley's mental hospital, where there are some terrible mental patients, maybe after recovering, they are waiting for life imprisonment or execution. One such psychiatrist, whose family he is accused of at the moment, told the court that he has lost his mental balance, and to this day he is a dangerous murderer. He needs psychiatric treatment. But he has been missing from the hospital for the last 15 days Where is he? Did he really run away or did he commit suicide? No response was received from Defense Intelligence. So, after calling Rudra Sen to solve the case, Rudra packed his bag. But from the day he came out, he had a high fever, and his head seemed to have doubled in weight. Somehow Sara came all the way to take medicine, I heard he will get an assistant, but where is he? So many roads have been crossed, no one has come.

Rudra was holding his breath inside, so he somehow came out and stood. As soon as he came out from inside, he saw thick clouds in the sky, it had rained a little earlier. There was a strong wind blowing over the river, and a little wet wind suddenly made his whole-body tremble. Somehow, he came out, trembling, and as soon as he came out, he saw a man standing outside, leaning on the railing of the launch, standing back, so Rudra could not see his face. Anyway, he went to the railing and stood beside him. The boy got busy when he saw him, raised his hand towards him and said"Good evening, I am Rajesh, Rajesh Sharma", Rudra shook the head and replied good evening, although he did not want to say much, he asked"I know you?"

Laughing softly, Rajesh replied,"Sir, I am your assistant. I have been sent to help you. When I came, I saw that you were sleeping and I heard that your body was not well, so I did not bother to call you anymore". Hearing this, Rudra smiled lightly and said"Hmm, I was told that someone was coming to help in this case, but I thought No one came". Rudra grabbed the pockets of his shirt and pants, and muttered,"Where did I put that?"

"What are you looking for?" Rajesh asked

..hmm, I think I left my cigarette inside"Rudra replied Rajesh handed the packet of cigarettes from his pocket to Rudra and said"And I have it, please sir" Rudra said"thanks for the cigarette", and then he grabbed a lighter from Rajesh and said with a long pull"Do you have any information, how long will it take?"

... which I heard for another fifteen minutes." Rajesh replied

... river and jungle wide area, how did the prisoner escape with the security and defense?"

... Sir, this question is in me as well, although I have never been here, but as far as I have heard about this place, not a very straightforward escape from now on"

Rudra said pulling on a cigarette,"that everyone is behind everyone, even if he stays in that area, the rest of the doctors, nurses and other patients of the hospital will not be at all relieved."

Fifteen minutes passed as he spoke.

Rajesh said,"That's it, sir. Sir, it seems that everyone is standing there for us."

Rudra saw a vast area of greenery, a huge wilderness surrounded by dense jungle. He saw a military jeep in front of the jetty, and in front of him are two men in military uniforms. The launch slowly landed on the jetty. As soon as Rudra and Rajesh got off the launch, an army officer approached them

..Good evening, I am Colonel Singh, the Chief Security Officer here. Are you EX Lieutenant Rudra Sen?" Singh greeted with a show of hands.

Rudra smiled and replied"Absolutely right, EX, now I am DIA agent Rudra Sen, and yes, he is with me Rajesh Sharma."

Colonel Singh told both of them to come in his jeep. There is a long way to go and even in the evening there is a storm, we have to go through the jungle, so no one has time to waste. As the sun goes down, the jungle takes on a strange magical form, as if some unknown mystery is engulfing them. Hidden somewhere is the lost insanity intoxicated with death.

3

After crossing the jungle road, they entered the hospital campus. The large and strangely beautiful interior, although it is not very clear as it is an environment mixed with darkness and light, although it is not difficult to understand that the horrible environment outside is not very understandable when enter here from the jungle. Their jeep came and stopped in front of a huge building, It is clear that this building, all its craftsmanship was made by the British, if most of the army buildings and offices are all made by the British. Rudra and Rajesh got out of the jeep Before leaving, Singh said,"Mr. Rajagopalan Murthy is waiting in the right room. He is our deputy director of this hospital,and yes, don't spend too many nights here and there. The place is not good. If you try to do anything else, you will be in danger." He thanked Singh for delivering them and for warning them at the same time, Rudra and Rajesh walked through the corridor of the building and entered the house of the deputy director. Rajagopalan was sitting in his chair, saw them and came forward towards them, raised his hand and greeted them saying"welcome, welcome, Mr. Rudra, I was waiting for you, there was no problem on the way?"

.. No, nothing like that,"Rudra replied and introduced himself to Rajesh by extending his hand and said" This is Rajesh Sharma, DIA has sent him to help me"

.. OK, so good you see, Mr. Sharma" He raised his hand and shook hands with Rajesh.

Rudra pulled up the chair in front of Murthy, he said,"I don't understand a thing. It is such a protected area, there is a river on it, a vast area of jungle."

Murthy laughed and said" You yourself were at the front, you also took military training, tell me, Mr. Rudra, it is very difficult for an army, if he thinks he can escape?"

.. That's right, if you give me a little case details, it will be an advantage" Rudra said Rudra could not finish his speech, suddenly he got up and sat down again , thenMurthy hurriedly ran and put his hand on Rudra's shoulder and said"Are you all right?"

.. Yes, just turn my head a little"Rudra bowed his head and replied,

Murthy put his hand on his forehead and said"Mr. Rudra, you have a fever, and it is not below 101 at all."Rajesh stood on the other side of Rudra, and then he said to Murthy"He actually traveled with a fever, and now the fever has probably increased." The Murthy was busy and immediately brought a tablet shand a glass of water from the drawer of his table, and said,"Mr. Rudra, take it, you rest today, we'll talk tomorrow."Rudra took the medicine and stood up and said," I was going to talk to Mr. Nigam for a while."

Murthy said," He's the assistant director, and he's the last one here.So, I'll tell you now, please go to your room and rest, we'll talk tomorrow morning."With that, Murthy rang the bell from his table, and when the guard standing outside entered, Murthy called Raju and called out to someone. After a while a young boy Murthy said,"We have arranged for you to stay in one of our staff bungalows. I hope you will like it." Murthy told Raju to take them and show them where they were staying. Rudra and Rajesh came to their bungalow. Arranged two rooms in the bungalow Rajesh said to Rudra"Sir, if you say tonight, I can be in your room or you can be in my room, if you need any"

Rudra said there is no need, but he wants to be alone. Rajesh went to his room, after a long journey he was feeling tired. Rudra and Raju entered his room, Raju brought his bag, so he put it on a chair on the side of the room.

Rudra asked him"How long have you been working here?"

Raju bowed his head and replied"5 years"

... where have you been? Here?" Rudra asked

.. Yes, but my house is on the other side of the river"Raju said

... Hmm, hope you have the proper knowledge of all roads in the jungle?" Rudra asked

.. roughly sir,"Raju answered in a few words

... OK, that's you" Rudra told him before he left

Raju said that he would bring dinner here, but Rudra said that he would not eat anything, asked him to go to the next room and ask Rajesh. Raju shook the head and said goodbye.

"A nicely decorated room, a baby girl playing, and her mother running after her with a plate of food, the girl not holding on to her mother at all, the girl's smirk as if enlivening the whole environment. The bluebird sitting on the branch of the tree in front is watching them play, and laughing and eating. Suddenly the whole atmosphere seemed to vanish, a cover exploded, a fireplace with a puff of black smoke darkened everything, mother's blood-stained body fell to the ground and a little farther away the baby girl, her hand swallowed as if in the fireplace."

His whole body went cold twice Rudra woke up in shock, his whole body was wet with sweat, he was breathing fast, his throat was very dry. Drink a lot of water from the water bottle from the table next to the bed. Then he got down from the bed, slowly took the cigarette, opened the door of the room and stood on the outside balcony. What a dream, a recurring nightmare. When will he will be released from this dream? Rudra looked at his watch, it was three o'clock at night, he knew he would never sleep again, what an enchanting atmosphere the whole area had taken in the deep night darkness.

4.

The next morning, before tea and breakfast were over, Singh arrived in a jeep to take them to the office, where he was told that Assistant Director Mr. Nigam was waiting for them. And without wasting time, the two of them got into the jeep and left. Slowly the jeep reached the office building. The previous day it was not understood in the dark, all around is very beautiful, the whole area is surrounded by various kinds of flower gardens. Everyone is working there, some looking at them with a dumb look Rudra asked"Are these the people here who are undergoing treatment?"

Singh laughed and replied,"Yes, this is done with those who are a little healthy, and there are various kinds of work."

The jeep has already arrived in front of the office the day before After saying goodbye to Singh, Rudra and Rajesh entered the office .

Seeing them, Mr. Nigam stepped forward, raised his hand and said,"I'm Assistant Director Nigam, I wasn't here yesterday. How is your body now? I heard your body wasn't right."

..Yes, I had a little fever, now I am very healthy"Rudra replied

" Tell me Mr. Rudra, how do you want to proceed"

"I want to know a little bit about the fugitive." Rudra said

"Captain Shekhar Chopra, an effective soldier of our Kargil Battalion, but I don't know what happened, he set his whole family on fire. The court proved that he was mentally unbalanced, so he was sent here for treatment, you know, a strange thing, if you saw him at that time, you would not even realize that there was a mental disorder in him, but at one point, he would become terrified, and he would kill anyone who came in front of him. It would have been difficult to handle him, at a time when we had chained him and kept him one by one."

"Who would take care of him here?" Rudra asked

"He was already under the treatment of Dr. Kapoor, he can speak well about the treatment, and after seeing the food or everything Manohar"Nigam said in reply

"Who is this Manohar?" Rudra asked

"Manohar is actually the ward boy of Unit B,"said Nigam.

This time Rudra was silent for a while and said to Nigam," If you don't have any problem, can I take a cigarette?"

"Hey sure, no problem" said Nigam, then began to say to himself again" Look Mr. Rudra, you want any help, you will get all the help from us."

"Thank you, I need your help"Rudra finished his speech and pulled out a cigarette and said"I want to talk to all of you house staff once, and especially with Dr. Kapoor, because Shekhar was under his care."Rudra said

Nigam immediately agreed with him that he would take care of everything. Rudra was silent for a while and asked,"Well Mr. Nigam, do you have any patients here? The name is Rafiq Islam?"

Nigam thought for a while and replied"Hmmm, no, there is no one by this name?""..Think about it, there are so many patients, it is normal not to remember the name, can you understand once you check the register?" Rudra insisted so that Nigam could say something

"No Mr. Rudra, all the patients are at my fingertips, and a total of 80 patients, nothing to remember. But why are you asking?"Asked Nigam

" No, nothing like that. I got the news that someone by that name has come here for treatment. In fact, he is a special acquaintance of mine."Rudra replied.

After a while the Murthy entered the house, he came and stood right behind Rudra, then his hand on Rudra's shoulder and said"Mr. Rudra, how is your body now?" Rudra looked back at the Murthy and smiled and replied"It's much better now, your medicine really worked yesterday."

"Did you sleep at night?"Murthy asked.

Rudra was silent for a while and then said"Yes, it was."Nigam said to Murthy,"Murthy, they will talk to our house staff." Nigam said that he would talk to Dr. Kapoor himself. Rudra said he wanted to visit the whole area once. Nigam said there was no problem, but the weather was not good, so it would not be right to go to the forest at this time.

Rajesh came out and asked,"Sir, do you understand everything?"

"What do you think?" Rudra asked Rajesh in return

"I don't understand how he escaped from the security he had done so much?"Rajesh said

"Look, maybe he didn't run away, he's hiding in the jungle, and that's the security in charge here, which is what we found here the last day. Everyone has a fear or objection to going to the forest. What is there in this forest, Shekhar's panic? But that is unknown, or something else" Rudra said seriously.

Then he said to himself,"Rafiq is here, I know, but where?" Then he looked at the forest and said,"Which road in the forest leads to the river, do you remember?"

"No sir, I came in a jeep, then it came down in the evening, it was dark, I can't remember"Rajesh admitted straightforwardly that he doesn't remember some of his roads. But Rudra looked at the forest. He was looking for something, thousands of questions were forming in his mind about this forest. There is no other way but to escape through this road, or Shekhar is a murderer, is killing him the real disease? Then he is nothing less than a wild animal in the forest. Maybe he is hiding in this forest looking for a prey, Rudra looked at the forest for a while, then said nothing and started walking towards the forest. Rajesh did not understand what Rudra wanted. So, Rajesh kept running after him with his feet together, and kept asking where he was going. Rudra said that he would like to see the forest once. Rajesh was shocked, once he looked at the sky and said"Sir, look at the sky, the weather is not good, is it necessary to go today?"

Rudra stood a few feet away, then said,"I only want to look at the whole map once, by which I can now grasp the whole course of escape."

Rajesh wanted to explain to him that it is dangerous to walk here without permission, if a complaint goes to the headquarters, there will be a drag on the job. Rajesh was a little surprised to accept Rudra's stubbornness, but they went back without bothering about it. As soon as they did not go far, they saw a security guard Rudra took a cigarette from his pocket and walked slowly towards the security guard .Then he went to him and asked for a lighter, Rajesh was trying to understand what is the real purpose of Rudra. To give Rudra the matchbox, Rudra grabbed his cigarette and said,"It's raining, what will you do, I don't see any tent?"

The security guard said very politely,"No sir, I have a habit, I'll go under any tree."

"Hmmmm, will you have a cigarette?"The security guard agreed to ask Rudra, then gave him a cigarette and said"How long have you been posting here?"

"It has been almost two years, sir." The guard answered

"Where was you before?" Asked again

"Sir, at Barrackpur camp, the guard replied,

.."Okay, tell me one thing, when you have been here for so long, I think you can tell the whole story of Unit A and Unit B". Rudra asked,

This time Rudra's demand became clear in his head. The guard began to say,"Unit B 5 km north of the main office which is falling towards your forest and Unit B 5 km south of the main office.People in Unit B who are in a very dangerous mental state and those who are a little bit healthy, such as those you see in the garden, in the kitchen or in any small work, They are in Unit A."

"What's in Unit B? I mean, jungle or river, what's the connection?" Rudra asked

"nothing .."The guard replied

Without further ado, Rudra slowly walked towards his bungalow. Rajesh was silent for a long time, this time he couldn't stay any longer and said"Do you think Shekhar has escaped through that jungle road?"

Rudra looked at Rajesh, didn't answer, just thought of something, then said" Do you have a cigarette?"Rajesh was stunned, because he didn't think that the answer to his question could come. So he didn't say anything, Or maybe he couldn't say, just took the packet of cigarettes out of his pocket and handed it to Rudra. Rudra took a long pull on the cigarette and said"Let's go, we have to sit at home and think a little".

5.

The next morning Rudra and Rajesh came to the office. Murthy has brought all the house staff and nurses together Murthy has chosen a canteen in the office to talk to, naturally, she needs a little more space to sit with so many people. Anyway, without wasting time, Rudra started talking to everyone one by one. As he was talking, he suddenly saw a woman, behind everyone, she was sitting invisibly. Rudra was standing next to the Murthy, so Rudra came and gestured to the Murthy and asked him about the woman. Murthy said that she is Pratima Devi, head nurse of Unit B. When he finished talking to everyone, Rudra called Pratima Devi. There is a seriousness in a woman's appearance with age.

Rudra asked"How long have you been here?"

... 10 years,"said Pratima Devi,

" then you are a very old staff here,"Rudra said with a laugh"Do you see Unit B?""..Yes" Seriously short answer again

.. Living with such horrible mental patients, caring, not afraid of you?"Rudra asked

.. No, if I was scared I would quit my job long ago. The thing is, I am afraid of healthy people, not mental patients."This is the first time the she has said many serious things

.. How was Shekhar, did you think he could ever escape?" Asked Rudra

.. Shekhar was a strange patient, when he normal used to talk to me a lot, talk about his war front, home, everything, but when his mental problem started, it was really hard to hold him. He wanted to kill everyone, then maybe anyone would be in front of him. He will be killed. But it is unthinkable that he will ever run away." Then sheremained silent for a while, then began to speak again." If he is not given medicine, he will become frightened when, that is our fear, without medicine, many things can happen."

..How many patients are there in Unit B?" Rudra asked

.. 28 people"again short answer

.. Pratima Devi, Rafiq Islam is among these twenty-eight people?" Rudra asked.

She looked at Rudra with strange eyes for a while, then said"No, there is no one by that name here, at least not in Unit B."

..And in unit A?"Asked Rudra

.. I can't say that, but as far as I know, there is no one by that name" replied the Pratima Devi

Rudra told her to leave, whatever he asked, was done. As Pratima Devi left, the Murthy came and stood near Rudra, asking"Did you get anything?" Rudra sighed and said"No, nothing like that"

Rajesh came out and asked"Sir, tell me what you feel?"

Rudra took a cigarette and said very worriedly"I don't understand, there is a disturbance somewhere. Where did Shekhar go in such security, how did he escape, and no one noticed anything?"Suddenly he said to Rajesh," You better go, I'm coming."

Rajesh asked in surprise," But sir, where are you going, I'm not coming either?" Rudra said,"I will call you when you need me."

After walking, he reached the office of the unit below Unit B. Rudra entered the office. There was no one inside the office. He saw that the daily register was placed on the table in front of the patients. He looked around a little. Without wasting time, Rudra quickly counted how many patients there were. He noticed that the Pratima Devi was right. There were exactly twenty-eight people. He quickly wrote down the notebook in his pocket, then started looking for Rafiq Islam's name. Although he found the whole book, he could not find Rafiq's name anywhere. Suddenly a footstep came to his ears, Rudra hurried out of the house with the notebook fixed, decided to go to the unit once, but coming down in the evening, anyway, he has to finish work before nightfall. So, without wasting time, he started walking towards Unit A. He came a little bit. Suddenly Rudra looked back at the sound of a car horn.

He saw Singh standing behind the jeep and calling him with the horn. Rudra turned and approached Singh's jeep and said,"What's the matter, where are you patrolling?"

Singh laughed softly and said,"It's my job to patrol. But where did you come from, you are walking in unison, I have been honking for a long time."Rudra said a little embarrassed.

"I came here in need, and I was a little distracted."Then he said quietly for a while. Going towards unit A, if you have no problem, can you leave a little?"

.. Don't say that, please. Come on, I'm leaving" Singh laughed and agreed to let Rudra leave the unit A. It didn't take long for Singh to drop Rudra off and leave, Unit A and somehow the unit office. But Unit A was not empty, a middle-aged gentleman was sitting and working, Rudra went and stood in front of him. The gentleman looked at Rudra a little surprised, then asked"Tell me, can I help?" Rudra thought for a moment and said,"I was actually sent by Mr. Rajagopalan, looking at the patient's daily register." He said,"Can you help me?"

He took the register out of the drawer at the bottom of his desk.

Rudra was a little surprised to see the patient counting with his mind, so he asked the gentleman,"Is everyone's name registered here? You mean, like, saltines and their ilk, eh?"

The registered patient in Unit A is 39. This time he checked the book carefully to see if Rafiq's name was there. But I didn't find anything there either Rudra came out of Unit A thanking the gentleman with a smile. When he came out, he saw a deep darkness descending all around, the friendship of the black clouds of the sky with the darkness of time, as if it had created the magic of a conspiracy. Rudra began to think, a list of 80 patients had been sent, he had seen for himself, not only that, the Murthy's corporation had both said that a total of 80 patients were here. But here in unit A and B match 67 patients. So where are the other thirteen? Have they escaped, too? Or they are not alive now. Thinking about this, Rudra did not understand when he entered an unknown road in the dark. He regained consciousness when a drop of cold water suddenly fell on him. He looked up at the sky in surprise and saw a sudden downpour of rain. Then he looked around and didn't know where he was going to find the way to his bungalow. He looked back and saw that Unit A could not be seen, he had come a long way, but on the wrong road. After the rain water fell on the ground, the road became very slippery, Rudra was trying to find a way while walking, suddenly startled, in the deep darkness it seemed as if someone was standing under a tree in front of him. Wearing a white sari, open hair, someone of medium build, it is not so dark. The shadow came out from behind the tree like an incorporeal soul as if Rudra could no longer walk, he became speechless, he is staring at that shadow. After a while, a voice came from that shadow,"Come here." Rudra couldn't think of anything, but he walked towards the shadow, now his face was clear in front of him. An old woman, very thin, but it is understood that she still has impossible energy in her body, blue eyes and strange white complexion. He stared at Rudra for a while, then said,"Have you lost your way?" Rudra replied,"Yes, I was walking a little distracted, then the rain came, now I don't know where to go." You won't find anyone, there is no one here, run away"Rudra said" I don't understand what you are saying, who doesn't, don't do it? You know who I am?" The woman said"

6.

Rudra woke up in the morning for tea. The night was soaking wet in the rain, the head was probably so heavy load and with it the body was biting hands and feet. He told Raju to leave the cup on the table and go to the bathroom to freshen up. He came out of the bathroom and saw Rajesh sitting on the bed in his room with tea, Rajesh looked at Rudra and said"Good morning sir, maybe you were out last night." he wiped his faces with towel and said,"Yes, something happened last night. It might not have been so late if I had lost the road."

Rajesh was surprised and asked"I mean, which road?"

Rudra took the cup of tea in his hand and took a sip and said,"I went to Unit A tomorrow. I was coming to think of something. It rained heavily, I can't see which way I'm on, it's dark and it's raining."

Rajesh asked curiously" What did you do then?"

Rudra sipped his cup of tea again and said," It's a strange thing. I'm looking for a way out. Suddenly I met with an old woman in a white robe."

.. In the rain? Who was there?"

Rudra laughed and said," No one will stand in that rain except the mad people, but he told me which way to go would be to my advantage, and kept telling me, run away from now on, it's not a good place"

... What are you saying? Sir, what do you think, who was it?" Rajesh asks,

This time Rudra walks and puts the finished cup of tea on a table in the room, then grabs a cigarette. Leaving the cigarette smoke, he said anxiously,"The question is not who the woman was, the question is, what did she want to say?"

.. what do you think, someone is trying to scare you?"Rajesh asked with a frown

... maybe someone is warning me, and the fear is on his own" he quiet for a while, then said"But in reality, there are sixty-seven people, so where are the other thirteen, are they lost in the jungle or have they merged into the river?"

.. What are you saying sir?"Rajesh asked in surprise

.. Shekhar was in Unit B, there were supposed to be twenty-seven matches, because twenty-eight patients, one missing," Rudra turned to Rajesh and asked"What, is that so?"

.. that's is right"Rajesh replied

.. but funny thing, the record of the mill says the calculation of twenty-eight." Rudra answered with a light smile and Rajesh went to ask some more questions but suddenly there was a loud knock on the door and both of them looked at the door. Singh came. He laughed and said"Good morning"

.. Good morning, but are you here this morning?"Rudra asked in surprise

.. Yes, the director sent me here to give an urgent message" Singh said

.. Tell me about it?"Rudra asked

.. I can't say that. But they have a meeting from eleven o'clock. You have been asked to meet him once before, so if you say so, I am waiting, you get ready, I have brought the jeep, I am letting you go,"said Singh.

"Thankyou, Mr. Singh, Then give me some time, I'll be ready in half an hour."Rudra replied, then Singh said that he was waiting outside with the jeep. Rudra and Rajesh hurried to get ready and went to the washroom.

In twenty minutes, they were both ready. Then he reached Singh's office in Singh's jeep as soon as he entered, he saw a crowd of people in the house besides Nigam and Murthy, as soon as he entered the room, Nigam noticed Rudra and hurried towards him. He said,"Come on, Mr. Rudra, I have been waiting for you." Then he stood beside Rudra and said to everyone,"Please gentlemen, may I have your kind attention, Mr. Rudra, a DIA agent and his assistant Mr. Rajesh, they have come here for a special investigation,"he said and introducing with everyone like Dr. Kapoor, Dr. Patnaik, and Dr. Burman. This time Nigam opened up a bit and explained the reason for calling them, Nigam started saying"Today is actually Dr. Kapoor's fifth wedding anniversary, so, on that occasion, he has a party in his bungalow today. His request is that you also come to his bungalow in the evening."

Rudra laughed and said"I will definitely come, why not come."

Dr. Kapoor raised his hand and said to Rudra,"I have invited everyone to this hospital, and you are our guests here, so, you are specially invited to my party."

Rudra pleaded,"Please, don't say that, we'll get there." As soon as Dr. Kapoor thanked him and left, Murthy approached Rudra, then grabbed Rudra's elbow and brought a corner of the room and said"Mr. Rudra, what are you doing?"

Rudra was a little surprised and asked with a frown,"I don't understand."

"... Mr. Rudra, it is a crime for you to go anywhere or collect documents without permission, as I said before, but you did it."

.. How did I do that?"

"You went to Unit B yesterday and then checked the documents there."

Rudra was a little surprised, how did he know, because there was no one when he went to Unit B, how did he know, then what did Singh say suspiciously? Because on the way back, I met Singh and Singh left him at the unit. Anyway, Rudra said"Don't mind, I actually thought about this little thing, didn't care so much, but I'll keep it in mind from next time."

"Hmmm, it's good for all of us." Nigam called out before he could finish.

Rudra realized that even though he was called to invite her, they all had a meeting here. So, Rudra came to Rajesh and said in a hushed voice"We have no more work here, their meeting will start, let's go".

7.

It was about eight o'clock in the evening, the party was in Kapoor's bungalow, Mozart or Beethoven was going on lightly, drinks and beautiful clothes were scattered all around. The open garden in front of the bungalow is beautifully decorated, with meals arranged on a table on one side and a bar counter on the other. Well-dressed waiters go around drinking, women getting overwhelmed on their makeup and husbandsdiscussion, and boys trying to tell each other stories of their own heroism. In fact, the fun of the party is that everyone is trying to convince everyone, but no one is listening or understanding.

Rudra and Rajesh arrived at the party, looked around once and saw that Nigam and Murthy had reached there long ago. Dr. Kapoor was talking to them, his eyes fell on Rudra, he quickly came forward with his hands"Please, welcome Mr. Rudra and Mr. Rajesh, come on, it's so late, everyone has come a long time ago."

Rudra laughed and replied," Usually, a party like this starts a little late at night, so I thought I'd come back in a little while."

"That's in your town, there's nothing here, so if you think there's going to be a party, you have to start a long time ago,"he said with a smile,"and especially the bar counter first."

Rudra laughed, brought a champagne as a gift, trying to give it to Kapoor, Kapoor said,"What are you doing, not me at all, come here first" and brought Rudra and Rajesh in the middle of a group of women.

He came and called to a woman from behind,"Darling, look here."

The woman turned and looked at Kapoor and looked at Rudra and Rajesh. Kapoor introduced her,"Darling, this is Mr. Rudra Sen, DIA, they have come here for an investigation, and he is Mr. Rajesh, his assistant. And this is my wife Mrs. Shelley Kapoor", Rudra smiled and handed the gift to her" Congratulations".

Shelley thanked and accepted the gift.

Kapoor smiled and said,"Darling, he gave me the gift, I said no, it should be given to the one who deserves it."

Mrs. Kapoor said with a smile,"Yes, that's right, those who endure their husbands all year round, their attitude means they deserve the gift of the day, what does Mr. Rudra say?"

Rudra smiled and said"I am a guest, why do you create animosity?"

Everyone laughed when he heard his answer, Kapoor said"but it's like Perfect Intelligence". Suddenly a call came from inside the crowd for Dr. Kapoor, he said"You guys talk, I'm coming a little".

Kapoor left with permission from Rudra, Shelley Kapoor slowly approached Rudra and said"Your job is interesting, James Bond type, isn't it?"

..Not at all, you can say before I used to save the country by fighting the external enemy, now I do the internal"

..so, how long have you been here?"

..well, until the case is settled"

..then come to my bungalow one day, I will hear the story from you"

..Okay, I will definitely come"

After talking for a while, when someone called Mrs. Kapoor, so, she left with Rudra's permission. Rudra looks at Shelly Kapoor, Shelly Kapoor, medium build, fair, short haircut, and eyes are light blue, all in all, the woman is very attractive.

Rajesh comes with two glasses of drinks to go Shelly Kapoor. Standing next to Rudra, he said to Rudra with a glass" There is an age difference between Dr. Kapoor and Mrs. Kapoor, a lot."

..Yes, so the victim is too big for the wife"Rudra replied with a sip of the glass of drinks.

While talking to Rudra Rajesh, he suddenly noticed that someone was looking inside from behind a tree just outside the bungalow. Rudra noticed better that he was trying to find something inside and out. He finished the glass with a sip and said to Rajesh,"If you don't mind, will you bring me a drink?"

..Of course, I'm bringing it now"

When Rajesh left, Rudra came out of the bungalow without saying anything to anyone, avoiding everyone's eyes, then very anxiously reached the place where the man was standing. Even though there was light inside, the place was very dark, he slowly followed him. He came and stood up, then said"Who are you, looking for someone?"

The man turned around and looked at Rudra, Rudra was startled, hey, That's the old lady I met that rainy night. Rudra was surprised, so he asked"Are you here? Looking for someone?"

The woman stared at Rudra again, as if with an exploding gaze she brought her face very close to Rudra's, then said"Yes, I was looking for you".

Rudra was even more surprised, he asked in surprise"Me? But why?"

... I said, go away from now on, why haven't you gone yet?"

..I'm here to answer some questions, I can't go anywhere until I get them."

This time she laughed again, then said,"Ask who the question is, I have the answer to one of the questions."

..what are you saying, I don't understand anything" Rudra got upset

..I have a puzzle? You must be stuck in a maze, no answer here"

"I am looking for somebody but can't find"Rudra said with some hope

... Who are you looking for? Yours? Is everyone here looking for that?" The woman smiled lightly and replied

... I am looking for Rafiq, do you know him? " Rudra asked the question with the hope of an answer in his mind

Rafiq? Is there? Surviving? Tied up? Unit B, cell number 42, what will happen to him?" The woman asked the question along with the answer

..I want some answers from her"

.. you can't find any answer, the answer is unknown to everyone, it's just their own question"said the woman with a smile.

Suddenly from behind it seemed that someone called his name, Rudra looked back and saw Rajesh coming and standing, Rudra took some time away from him and when he looked in front again he saw that there was no one there.

Rudra looked desperately for the woman, but did not see her. Like that mysterious night here, that woman is also a mysterious one, but why did she come to him, what did he want to say? Concerned, Rudra came back to Rajesh with a thousand questions in his mind, seeing him.

Rajesh asked"What are you doing here sir, everyone inside is looking for you".

When Rajesh came back to the party with Rudra, Murthy came forward towards Rudra, then said"Do you feel bad?"

..No no, I'm fine"

..then I couldn't see you, I thought you were feeling bad"

.. no, I was just having a headache"

..I would rather tell Dr. Kapoor that there must be some medicine in his house"

.No no, you don't have to be busy, I'd rather go to my room a little, I'll see you tomorrow"

Meanwhile Dr. Kapoor and Nigam have come to them, Dr. Kapoor said very worriedly"iseverything all right? Mr. Rudra, are you alright?"

..Yes, a little headache, I'm taking permission from you, you don't have to be worry"

..But you didn't have dinner either"Dr. Kapoor said

..no problem, please continue" Rudra went out of the party

Rajesh came and said"Come on sir, I will deliver you"

Rudra said he would have no problem, he could leave, and there was a jeep outside so he could leave.

8.

The next morning, Rudra was having tea in the garden, as if he was suffocating inside the house, so the softness of the morning seemed to him more peaceful than the mystery of the night. Rajesh came to the verandah with a cup of tea and saw Rudra sitting in the garden, so he slowly came to Rudra and said"Is the body all right now?"

..Yes, the body has been in trouble since the day I came."

..Yes, I noticed that too, so what's the plan for today?"

Rudra stood up on the garden bench with the cup of tea, then said"I will go to the forest today, get ready quickly".

Rajesh said a little hesitantly"But sir, you need permission to go there".

Rudra said,"It doesn't matter, if you listen to their rules in all matters, the real work will not be done, you will understand"

…But sir, didn't you see the day before, Rajagopalan idol told you, if there is any problem?"

Rudra got angry and said to Rajesh,"You have not been sent here to help me to take care of their rules?" Then he stepped forward and said,"If you want to go with me, I'll give you fifteen minutes. Get ready, or I'll go alone."

Rajesh saw that Rudra was not listening in any way today, so he took a little time to get ready.

Not in fifteen minutes, it took them half an hour to get out. Rudra started walking along the road of the forest with Rajesh, what a thumping environment of the forest even during the day. There are some small trees standing by the hands of the huge tall trees, and a lot of tall grass, as if Shekhar would come running from behind with a knife. The two of them continued to keep an eye on the surroundings. After walking a long way, a strong wind started blowing. The whole forest seemed to be in turmoil. In that voice they could not hear their own voices. Somehow shouting, Rudra pointed to the front and said,"The wind is coming from that front, do you understand that side of the river?"

The wind was blowing and with it all the leaves and twigs of the forest began to fly randomly towards them, Rajesh said"Sir, the storm has risen, nothing can be seen in front", before it was over it rained in torrential downpours In the rain, together with a handful of unknown deaths, Rajesh told Rudra,"The road to the river has been found, but the way back seems to be lost."

Rudra realized that they had come a long way but it would be difficult to return, as the storm and the torrential rains had led them astray. Rudra started walking some distance, the dry leaves of the forest with his eyes and some dust started flying from nowhere. The rain water soaked them over half After walking some distance like this, Rajesh suddenly saw a broken house in his eyes.

He shouted at Rudra,"Sir, look over there, it looks like you can take shelter there, at least until the weather is fine."

Obeying Rudra Rajesh's words, both of them escaped and reached the broken house. A white broken house, almost in ruins, somehow the two of them pushed open the door and went inside. The storm came into the house through the open door and began to fall Rajesh somehow locked the door from the inside with all his strength This time their eyes fell on the inside of the house Rudra looked around and said"It's a very old church, but in the jungle?"

Shaking his clothes, Rajesh said,"God Himself knows what is hidden in this world."

Rudra took a cigarette out of his pocket, then said,"There's something hidden, in this deep forest and the river is a witness to the conspiracy made by this hospital."

... I mean, what about the conspiracy to lose Shekhar?"

..Very normal, look, according to our records, there are eighty patients and in reality sixty-seven patients, so where are the other thirteen?" Then why haven't you searched for so long? And who is that old lady who keeps coming to me to tell me to leave now, and then where is she going? I can't even see him at night."

.. but sir, what is he trying to say?"

... I don't know, but he told me that Rafiq is here"

This time Rajesh was very curiously said"I don't even know who he is, and what he has to do with this case."

Rudra stared at Rajesh for a while, as if some past suddenly began to wander in his memory in the form of reality in front of him, Rudra said"Rafiq used to see the maintenance of all the bungalows in our camp. He would go to my house for whatever reason, help my wife when she needed it, I had a little girl, and she became good friends. I was posting outside most of the time, even then I was out, no one will know that he came to my house and proposed to my wife differently My wife disobeyed, kicked him out of the house, saying that if he ever came here again, he would complain in his name. He leaves, but remembers the blaze of insults, the flames of revenge, then one day, at noon, when my wife was sleeping in the house with my daughter, he enters the kitchen, turns on the gas, burns them to death. They were burned to ashes, I didn't even recognize them."

With Rudra's eyes water started coming down, the sound of his throat kept coming Rajesh was listening to everything with unblinking eyes, as if"then" came out of his mouth.

Rudra regained his composure, wiped away the tears and said,"Rafiq was caught, but the court found that he was mentally unbalanced, in need of treatment, and would be hanged when he recovered. I got the news that he had been sent here, so I told him Finding out here".

Rajesh said this time"But sir, there is no Rafiq's name in any of the records, how can you find it"

Rudra replied,"That's the wonder, why not, and I have the news, Rafiq is in the unit B."

The word might have gone a little further, but suddenly a voice came to their ears from outside The sound of so many horns, looking for them with a small mic from outside Without opening the door, I heard Singh from inside the door saying,"Mr. Rudra and Mr. Rajesh, I know you are inside, the weather is not good outside, it is dangerous to stay here, please come out".

Rajesh hurriedly said to Rudra,"Sir, what are you going to do this time? They understand that we are here, and we are in the forest without permission."

Rudra said,"No need to say anything, come on, open the door and go out quietly with him, I'll see later."

Rudra and Rajesh opened the door of the church and came out. They saw Singh standing in front of the jeep. Without saying a word, they both got into the jeep and got up. Singh turned the jeep around and drove through the jungle, the storm was over, there was no rain anymore.

Singh said,"You didn't come here at this time without telling anyone."

Rudra and Rajesh looked at each other once, but did not answer.

9.

Rudra was standing in the garden in the morning sipping a cup of tea as usual. The rays of the first sun in the morning and the softness of the morning air calms his restless mind, even if only for a while. The fragrance of the morning bird's feathers and the blossoming flowers reminds him of a strange sanctity. The work of unrighteousness and impurity that he is engaged in, let it go out of his mind in an instant. Mrs. Kapoor suddenly caught his eye as soon as he started feeling the morning. The morning walker has opened the door of her bungalow garden and is coming towards her with a smile. He smiled and said good morning and stood in front of her, then said"Do you wake up at such a time every day?" Rudra laughed and replied"Yes, a very old habit".

"I go jogging along this road in the morning, I saw you today, so I went in to say good morning to you."

"Well done, drink this morning tea with me, what's the problem?"

"Sure, I have no problem."

Rudra called Raju and asked him to bring two cups of tea, then to ask Mrs. Kapoor, Mrs. Kapoor said, it is better to have tea sitting in this garden, because the morning is very beautiful. Mrs. Kapoor sat on a bench in the garden and said,"Mr. Rudra, you left early that day. I heard later that you were ill. I was very worried. What happened that day?"

"It's been pretty long since I've been here. Nothing, just a headache and a fever at night."

Mrs. Kapoor said anxiously,"It's either a good sign, you show me a doctor."

Rudra laughed and said,"There is no doctor in everyone's house anymore!"

Mrs. Kapoor laughed and replied,"That's funny. You know, there's one thing you don't drink alcohol yourself."

Rudra asked in amazement"I don't understand"

Mrs. Kapoor leaned lightly on the garden bench and said"Where is his time, to see if I feel sick, he is busy with his work, and everything else ..." Mrs. Kapoor fell silent.

Rudra said,"What's the matter, even though he's busy, you have a lot of friends here, time is running out."

Mrs. Kapoor smiled contemptuously and said"Friend? Okay?"

Rudra went to ask Mrs. Kapoor in return, whoever she said like that, then Raju came in front of them with tea, Raju went to ask Rudra to leave with tea, then Rajesh came with a cup of tea. Rajesh came and saw Mrs. Kapoor and said good morning and asked"How long have you been?"

Mrs. Kapoor laughed and replied"A long time, I see your senior is having fun alone in the morning, so I left to give him some company" Rajesh laughed and said"you have done well, he needs some company."

Mrs. Kapoor said,"you guys, just carry on, it's time for me to leave. Dr. Kapoor will come out, he will have to get his breakfast ready."

Rudra and Rajesh stood up and said goodbye to Mrs. Kapoor. Before leaving, Mrs. Kapoor said,"Some things may be left unfinished. The next tea party will be at my house. The words will be completed that day. Bye."

After saying goodbye to Mrs. Kapoor, Rudra came back to Rajesh. Rajesh then finished his tea and lit a cigarette and sat on the bench. Seeing Rudra, he said,"we have to go to the main office. Nigam called, told me not to find you. Today you can talk with Manohar, and Dr. Kapoor is also free after twelve, so you can talk."

After a while, both of them came to the office of Nigam. When he reached the office, he saw a middle-aged gentleman standing there with a bald head, Nigam approached them and said"This is Manohar Bakchi, this is in charge of Shekhar's cell".

Rudra came forward towards Manohar, then said"How long have you been in charge of the unit, Manohar?"

"It's been almost four years."

"How is Shekhar's escaped?"

Manohar rolled a little, he looked at the Nigam once in fear, then cried and said"Believe me sir, I don't know how he escaped, I just gave him food and medicine"

Rudra brought his face close to hers and put his eyes on hers and said"He told you all about his family, all his mind, even said that he will run away from now on, he has some work to do." Frightened by Manohar, Rudra continued to say to him,"Am I wrong, Manohar?"

Manohar cried in fear, he kept saying"Sir, I thought, crazy delirium, I didn't care then, forgive me"

Rudra shook his head and said"It was necessary to pay attention, Manohar. Not all madness is equal."

Manohar said"I have made a mistake, sir"

Rudra asked this time"What did he say, where will he go? Where did he say to run away?"

"He didn't say anything to me, believe me," he began to cry, then said,"I didn't ask either, because asking too many questions would have been awful."

Rudra said"Okay you can come,"

For so long Rajesh and Nigam were both watching like silent spectators. As soon as Manohar left, Nigam asked Rudra,"How did you know so much?"

Rudra smiled lightly and replied,"It is my job to know everything or to know everything, Mr. Nigam."

After a while, Dr. Kapoor came to the house and without understanding anything, he said to the Nigam,"Did you call me?"

Nigam said,"Yes, actually Mr. Rudra has some queries from you."

"Oh, of course," he said, turning to Rudra."Tell me what you want to know, but first tell me how is your body now? I was a little upset that day, to leave your party suddenly."

Rudra laughed and said,"Yes, I'm fine now. I've been suffering from this fever and headache for a long time now."

Dr. Kapoor said,"But you need a little checkup, because I don't understand what's going on these days."

Without wasting time, Rudra asked,"Dr. Kapoor, you used to treat Shekhar, what exactly was his problem?"

"What he had was LBD symptoms, I mean, let's say hallucination, living as someone else. You'll see in front of him what might not exist. This is LBD, which in our medical language is called Levi's Body Dementia. But Shekhar had hallucinations, he would see someone else, someone he didn't like, and would rush to kill him."

"Was it possible for Shekhar to recover?"

"Needless to say, these are long-term treatments."

Rudra pleaded with a little"I will not ruin you for a long time, one last question, I heard Shekhar was punished for killing his family, is this disease the reason for his murder?"

Dr. Kapoor said very calmly,"There is no doubt about it, or what we have heard is that he was living a happy family, there was nothing wrong, that's the reason for this."

Rudra thanked Dr. Kapoor and said goodbye, then said to Nigam,"It is not possible for Shekhar to escape with such a heavy guard. I think he is hiding somewhere near this jungle or river. It may be dangerous for ten others, but the bigger problem is his own life is not safe also."

10.

Life, this life is big and diverse. The rainbow in the sky also adapts to the character of man. What is seen in front is not true, and what is true may never come to the fore. There are books that kill people if they fall in front of wild animals in the forest, but the creature called man, he will come and harm people in any way, maybe even God himself does not know that. In a word, God was very happy after creating this beautiful world, but in creating human life, he regretted that he had created his own creation to destroy it. Violence, hatred, jealousy, selfishness is all around people.

Rudra has been thinking all the time, Rafiq is in Unit B, but how to meet him. When he reaches Unit B, he will never achieve his goal by hiding like this. Rudra could not understand what was happening, as if his head had started to ache again since morning. Rajesh came out in the morning and said that if there is no work today, he will visit the entire campus once. Rudra's body had been feeling bad since morning, so he didn't want to go out anymore.

Rudra was sitting in the garden lighting a cigarette, looking for answers to various questions, many mysteries to unravel, but did not understand anything. Suddenly Raju comes out of his room. He came to the garden and said to Rudra,"Sir, your phone is inside." As Rudra was distracted, he stared at Raju for a while.

Raju didn't understand the meaning of his gaze, so he said again"Sir, your phone is inside, what can I say? Are you busy?"

This time Rudra became normal and said"Oh no no, I don't have to say that, I'm coming." This time Rudra hurried to his room to pick up the phone, saw Raju put down the receiver of the phone, picked up the receiver to his ear and said"Hello, I am Rudra Sen".

A female voice came from the other side saying"Mr. Rudra, I am Mrs. Kapoor"

"Hey yes, tell me, how are you?"

"Well, are you busy?"

"No, I'm a little free today, tell me."

"Then why don't you come to my bungalow once, I would talk a little," Then she said a little hesitantly,"If you have no problem."

Rudra was silent for a while and then said,"Okay, I'm trying."

Mrs. Kapoor was very happy to hear that Rudra was coming. Mrs. Kapoor said,"Just five or six bungalows from your bungalow, DA 40. Come on, I'm waiting."

Rudra said that he was coming a little later and put down the phone. Putting down the phone, Rudra started thinking that he had said that he would go, but would he really go? Is it okay to go? Then he realized to himself that he was probably thinking a little too much.

It took ten minutes on foot to reach Rudra's Mrs. Kapoor's bungalow, Rudra reached there without coming or not coming. The bungalow is very beautiful, and most of all as beautiful as it is, it has been kept beautiful Arriving at the bungalow, Mrs. Kapoor rang the doorbell and came out to fasten the rope of her house coat.

He opened the door and looked at Rudra with a smile and said"Truth be told? I didn't expect you to come" Rudra laughed and replied"Actually I was getting bored too".

"Come in"

Rudra went in and Mrs. Kapoor closed the door. The outside of the bungalow is as beautiful as the inside. The beautifully decorated glass table placed in the middle of the room and surrounded by two large wooden sofas, the huge painting room in the room has greatly enhanced their level of artistic taste.

Rudra went and sat on one corner of the sofa and Mrs. Kapoor sat very comfortably on another sofa just opposite him. Then he laughed and said"Mr. Rudra, tell me what to take, tea, coffee or something else"

Rudra asked"Anything else?"

"I mean whiskey, ram, vodka is all there, Army Doctor's house, you'll get everything." Laughing, Mrs. Kapoor immediately said,

"Oh no no, not at all, no drinks at this time. I'd rather have a coffee at this time."

"As you say," Mrs. Kapoor called her housekeeper Deendayal for two cups of coffee. As soon as Deendayal came and shook his shoulder.

Rudra said"Mrs. Kapoor, what were you saying that day?"

"Tell me," asked Mrs. Kapoor, frowning

"I mean, not everyone here, something like that."

"Oh, yeah, hey, if there's such a party here, it's for everyone, in fact no one, do you understand?"

"Oh, I understand," said Rudra in silence, then he was just going to ask to Mrs. Kapoor"Well, Mrs. Kapoor ..." Suddenly Rudra noticed when Mrs. Kapoor was on the same sofa next to him.

Mrs. Kapoor stopped him and said,"It's not good to hear Mrs. Kapoor ten times, call me Shelley."

Rudra said a little uncomfortably"but Mrs. Kapoor ..."

Shelley said,"There's a lot of talk inside, I'm alone, you're looking at that mirror," she pointed to a mirror, then said,"My daily companion, I talk to her every day, she doesn't answer, but she listens to me." Shelly could not finish the word, Deendayal put coffee on the table. Shelley said that she would make her own coffee. When Deendayal left, she made coffee and handed the cup to Rudra. Then he took a cup and sipped it and said,"There is no one who will listen, understand or explain. It's really hard to understand what the pain of loneliness is, Mr. Rudra."

Rudra said"Why, can you tell Mr. Kapoor?" Shelley laughed, then said,"His time is worth more than me, the hospital, patients and along with nurses, lady doctors"

"What are you saying?" Rudra asked in surprise

She laughed, she leaned back on the sofa and said,"I know everything, but I have nothing more to say. I just wanted a friend to whom I could share everything."

Rudra went on to say"But Mrs. Kapoor ...",

Shelley didn't let the word end, she came very close to Rudra and put her finger on Rudra's lips and said"I told you, Shelley" then she gently lowered her hand from her lips and placed it on Rudra's chest and said"Will I be looking for that thousand day friend?"

Rudra was more uncomfortable this time, he was trying to say a lot to remove himself, but Shelley was sitting in such a place on his chest, Rudra could not say anything more."It's not right, Shelley."

Shelley gently unbuttoned Rudra's shirt, Rudra repeatedly said,"What are you doing, it's not right."

Shelley rubbed Rudra's open chest with her soft lips and tongue, Rudra realized that he was about to lose himself this time, it's been a long time, a woman has touched his body like this. Rudra doesn't understand who he is, begging himself or this woman, who is begging him for an impossible sexual thirst. Shelley slowly lowered her hand from Rudra's chest and started rubbing Rudra's penis with her hand over his pants. Then she rubbed her lips near Rudra's neck and put her lips on Rudra's lips and started kissing him for a long time. Gradually Shelley's breath merged with Rudra's breath. She could not understand when Rudra's hand came off Shelley's house coat and touched her exposed chest. Shelley got up, then took Rudra's hand and led him to the bedroom. She puts Rudra on the bed, then throws her house coat on the floor, sits on Rudra, takes off his pants and throws them on the floor. Then she took Rudra's open penis inside her vagina and both of them became intoxicated with sex urge. In a primitive game, both of them get together, as if the desert that has not seen a drop of rain for a long time has suddenly come down.

11.

Rudra was not sleeping that night either. He had never imagined before he would come here that he would be met in such a way that anyone would meet him again with his body's lost needs. He could not understand how right and what was wrong. But when Shelley's body merged with his body, he realized it was clear that his closed eyes were on his wife.

Although Shelley quenched her body's thirst, Rudra did not realize that he had quenched his own thirst, but a strange feeling was at work in him, perhaps this desire was dormant in him, not at all.

Rudra has been lying awake for a long time, as if he has fallen asleep from his two eyes forever. Lying after the clock is his old habit So he looked at the clock once, it was about two in the night, and how long can he sleeps in these sleepless eyes? Rudra came out of the room with a cigarette and stood on the balcony. The night is not as enchanted with mystery as it is today. A cold wind seemed to touch his mind again and again, cigarette smoke was billowing into the sky. Suddenly he looked at the tree in the garden again, as if he was looking at it, he tried to see if someone was really standing or if he was wrong. The old woman came and stood in front of the tree to try to see a little better. Seeing him, he came running down from the balcony.

"You? Here? Now?"

The old woman looked at him with that fixed gaze and said,"I have no reason or time to go or come anywhere." Then she looked at the sky once, then said,"you look everyday the night, have you ever talked to the night?"

"What do you mean by night?" Rudra asked in surprise

"All the stars in the sky are covered by the light of day, but at night they appear, somehow? Who knows the deep night, their real identity" the woman continued to smile, the smile was very mysterious.

A strange shiver ran through Rudra's blood as he heard the smile, but it was clear to him that the woman wanted to say something, so she somehow forced out her resentful voice,"What do you mean?"

"Did you find Rafiq?"

"I know he's in Unit B, I'll take permission tomorrow morning."

The woman smiled again and said,"Permission? You will never get it. You are stuck, stuck in the circle of time."

"I mean?"

"Who are you, the one you were sharing your grief with all this afternoon?"

Rudra asked in surprise,"How did you know all this?"

The woman said in a very contemptuous tone,"Don't you have the answer to my question? So, you are asking me.", then he looked around and said,"Look around, there are a thousand questions hidden here, find the answers. But I know, you can't, because the biggest question is you, you haven't found yourself yet, have you?"

Rudra did not understand what the woman was talking about in the enigma. His head suddenly felt as if someone had made him very heavy, an impossible pain seemed to be starting again, his heart was beating very loudly. His voice was muffled, but somehow Rudra asked"Who are you?"

"Me?" The woman began to laugh, a laugh, the sky trembled. The gentle breeze that had been giving her mind a beautiful feeling a while ago, seemed to have stopped in fear at that laugh, Rudra could hear nothing but that laughter. The woman smiled in front of his eyes and seemed to fade away It was as if the woman was taking away her breath, her feelings, her desires, everything. Gradually a thick black darkness surrounded Rudra, which was impossible for Rudra to break through.

When Rudra's eyes opened, Rudra was in the hospital bed. Gradually his vision became clear Kapoor, Rajesh and Murthy are standing in front. As soon as Rudra tried to sit up straight, Kapoor came and said,"Hey, don't be too busy, lie down, rest."

Murthy also agreed with him and said"Dr. Kapoor is right, you need rest. What happened or happened, we will discuss later. I was very worried, now that you have regained your senses, I am a little relieved."

Rudra lay down and said to Murthy,"Mr. Murthy, I need permission to go to Unit B" Murthy was very surprised and said,"But why Unit B?"

"Because Shekhar was there, and I really want to see that place,"

Murthy said,"Actually, no one has the right to enter Unit B without a doctor. If you get permission, someone will get it for the first time. So, I will try."

Rudra said with a soft smile,"How many patients have escaped from you now, Mr. Murthy?"

Murthy said very seriously,"I understand, so I said, I will try, but I can't commit, Mr. Rudra, forgive me."

He looked at Kapoor and said,"Dr. Kapoor, I have a very important job. I'm going out. If there's any need, let me know."

Raja Gopalan Murthy said goodbye to everyone after being relieved by Kapoor. Rudra said something to Rajesh, but Kapoor kept quiet in front of him, then looked at himself and saw that he was dressed as a patient. So, Rudra was very upset and asked Kapoor,"Who changed my clothes?"

The doctor laughed and replied,"The nurse here."

Rudra said with equal annoyance,"It may be a pleasure to you, but not to me. And why have I been wearing in this garment, am I your little patient here?"

Kapoor laughed in the same way and said"This is our rule here, in this room, in this bed we have to wear this dress while lying down"

Rudra said"Oops, this is your rule."

Kapoor put his hand on Rudra's shoulder and said"You talk to your friend now, and allow me, it's time for me to look at other patents"

Rudra replied"Do you need permission to come or go?"

Kapoor went out laughing evenly, Rudra noticed him till the last moment of his departure, then said to Rajesh"come here sit, talk"

Rajesh came and sat on the bed next to him, then said"but sir, what happened last night? What did you do in the garden?"

Rudra said,"It's a long story, I'll tell you everything, but I'm sure they won't give permission."

Rajesh was surprised and said"But why?"

Rudra thought for a while and said,"Because, with permission, they will reveal a lot. There is a hidden truth here, which they want to hide."

Rajesh wanted to know"So what are you going to do?"

Rudra looked at the ring on his hand and said,"This is my wife's gift to me on my wedding anniversary." The answer to this question was very strange. He didn't find the words to say something, just stared at Rudra.

12.

The soft touch of a hand seemed to relieve the impossible headache. It is as if the finger of an artist is moving very slowly through the hair of his head, an obsession of love is trying hard, to give him a little sleep of peace. A hot breath came over his forehead, then he felt the touch of a soft lip on his forehead. Rudra's eyes opened; his wife was sitting near his head with her hands on his head. Rudra put his hand on his wife's hand and said"Are you here? How did you get here?"

Laughing softly, his wife replied,"Whenever you are sick, wherever I am, I have come to you and slept beside you. Have you forgotten, Rudra?"

Rudra placed his head on his wife's lap and said,"Where have you gone, I have become one."

Rudra's wife put her hand on Rudra's head and said"Where am I going to leave you? I am with you, by your side, always."

Rudra said,"Don't worry, I have found Rafiq. I will teach him exactly. He must be punished for what he has done and what he has done wrong."

Rudra's wife slowly walked away from him and walked towards the door, then turned to him and said,"You rest, I'm leaving for the day."

Rudra started shouting"No, don't go, stay with me, don't leave me."

Rudra's wife laughed and said,"Is that so? I am not allowed to stay here. Come on." As soon as he finished speaking, a fire was burning from under his feet, as if his wife had been burnt to ashes in a huge fire.

Rudra screamed and woke up. He could hear the sound of his own breathing. Rudra wiped his sweaty face with the bed sheet.

The next day Rajesh came and appeared early in the morning, the first question was"Sir, did you sleep at night?"

Rudra looked at Rajesh for a while in amazement, then said"Did I get a call?"

"No, is anyone supposed to call?" Rajesh asked very enthusiastically

Rudra paused and replied"No, not like that", then asked Rajesh"Which unit am I in?"

"It's not a unit, it's a general medicine center, where there's a fair amount of treatment, we're not here prior."

Rudra sat up straight on the bed and said"How much is Unit B from now on?"

Rajesh thought for a while and said"How long will it be, five minutes?"

Rudra was about to call Rajesh and say something, but suddenly he heard a good morning voice and turned around and saw that Dr. Kapoor had come with a smile. The first thing he said was,"I left all the patients and came to the hospital to see you first. How are you feeling now?"

Rudra smiled and replied"very good"

Kapoor himself started looking at Rudra with the stethoscope hanging around his neck, Rudra kept saying"I felt very bad thinking that tomorrow I have treated you very badly, don't mind, please"

Kapoor laughed. He smiled and said,"No, no, not at all. If we thought about it, we would have to give up medicine."

Rudra asked"How do you feel, all right?" Kapoor said,

"Yes, perfect, are the people in the army so weak?" Then he said again,"But you need a complete rest, a few more days."

"yeah fine, but can I go out a little? Do you understand, feel out of breath here" Rudra said in a slightly pleading tone.

Kapoor agreed, saying,"Okay, but don't stay out long, and come here and rest, okay?"

Rudra laughed and said,"Absolutely, don't worry."

Kapoor laughed and left. As soon as Kapoor left, Rudra got up from the bed quickly, then said to Rajesh"Do you have a cigarette?"

Rajesh said"Yes, there is"

Rudra slipped the slipper under the bed and said"Come on, let's go out".

Rudra came out with Rajesh, then took a cigarette from Rajesh, pulled it out and said,"Come on, there's no point in wasting time."

Rajesh was surprised and said"I mean? Where are you going?"

Rudra said very short"Unit B, which one would it be?"

Rajesh showed the direction of the road Rajesh and Rudra somehow appeared in front of Unit B. Rudra saw security standing below, Rudra realized that once he could be avoided, all his problems would be solved. Rajesh asked Rudra"Sir, we don't have any permission letter, how can you go inside?"

Rudra thought for a while and said to Rajesh,"Listen, you go first, go and get in touch with the security, take him to the side, I will go inside, I will find the rest of the cell number."

Rajesh did exactly as Rudra said, and Rudra got into Unit B after being a little distracted by the secret. Ascending the iron spiral staircase, the cells all around looked as if some wild animals had been captured there. There is very little light here, the dim light always indicates a terrible danger, Rudra keeps looking for one cell after another. He is so drunk looking for Rafiq's cell that he doesn't realize how far he has come. Seeing one cell after another, Rudra suddenly noticed the last cell. The inside of the cell is so dark that it is impossible to understand the real look. But Rudra tried to take a good look at that cell. There is a shadow leaning against the wall in the dark. Rudra called the shadow"Rafiq" with his hand on the cell wall.

The shadow did not answer, but in the darkness, it was understood that he turned his head and looked at Rudra once. Rudra kept saying,"If you keep yourself in the dark, you can't hide your identity, Rafiq. I'm here for you, come forward, come to the light, Rafiq."

The shadow was completely unresponsive, did not answer, just stood up and turned back to Rudra and went into more darkness. As if covering himself with more ambiguity Rudra shouted,"You have ruined my family, what have they done? How much the little boy loved you, you killed him so cruelly, come on, how many nights I have not slept for you. My family comes every night, asks me Why couldn't I punish their killer?"

This time the shadow suddenly turned around and ran towards Rudra, Rafiq's face became clear to Rudra. Rafiq grabs the grid and says to Rudra,"Look at me, look well, I have come in front of you, what will you do to me here, will you kill me? Will you take revenge? You can't do anything, but you will be finished."

Rudra asked in surprise,"What do you mean?"

Rafiq continued,"Yes, I killed your family, I did well. There was the Cargill war, everyone knows the reason, but all the Muslims were caught pretending to be Pakistani spies. I used to live a good life by doing ordinary work in army camps, who did I harm, but why was I looked at with suspicion, can you tell? Your wife said the same thing, your little girl also said one day, I am a spy, and I could not stand it, I burned it to ashes."He continued to laugh.

"You've finished everything for me, Rafiq."

"No, I didn't finish, I wouldn't have finished either, if I hadn't come here," said Rafiq."mean," Rudra asked.

Rafiq shouted,"It's a jungle, and we're all animals, every day is our prey, and everyone's making millions by selling us."

Rudra kept asking,"What do you mean, open up?"

Rafiq laughs and shouts, runs around the cell and says,"Understand, you'll understand, you're stuck."

The whole area trembled at Rafiq's shout, as if the sound of his laughter would break Rudra's ears and blood would come out this time. Hearing his screams, others from other cells also started shouting Suddenly it came to Rudra's ears that someone was calling his name, he turned around and looked down at the railing. Rajesh looks up from below and says to Rudra"Sir, come down quickly, the security is coming up with the whole team and Singh has come too".

Rudra heard and understood everything, but it was as if he had become numb, his hands and feet were numb, there was no answer to give him, Rafiq's words were floating in his ears, and his smile seemed to surround Rudra's brain. After a while, Rudra realized that he had lost the ability to walk straight, Singh and Rajesh came and grabbed him from above, but the next one was completely unknown to Rudra.

13.

Everyone forcibly grabbed Rudra and brought him to the room where he was lying. Rudra was in a state of obsession Everyone was talking but the ability to say or do something seemed to be taken away. With a faint gaze in front of his eyes, he realized that Kapoor had given him an injection and handed it to him, and in a few moments that faint light was shrouded in a sheet of darkness.

He doesn't know how long Rudra slept When he opened his eyes, he realized that the weight of his head had increased a lot, and even the slightest light had caused a strange burning sensation in his eyes. He could not sit up at all still tried to sit a little, He saw a nurse standing next to him, she said to Rudra"I'm helping, will you sit down?"

Then the nurse grabbed Rudra and put him on the bed, Rudra thanked her. After a while Rajesh arrived, then he saw Rudra and smiled and said"Thank God, if you wake up then".

Rudra was a little surprised and asked"How long am I sleeping?"

"How long?" Rajesh raised his eyebrows and laughed, then said"Perfectly woke you up after three days."

"What are you talking about?" Rudra was surprised, then said"What happened to me?"

"You went to Unit B and suddenly fell ill. The place was very dangerous. I was waiting outside after you went in, but you were late, seeing that, I decided to go inside, but the security would not let me in. Then I saw Singh crossing uninterrupted, I was forced to ask him and told him, so I could get inside with his help. Now I wonder if I was lucky enough to be in danger."

"That's it, I understand. Was Murthy or Nigam saying something?"

"Yeah, but he didn't tell me much, he said he would talk to you."

Rudra tried to sit up straight, then said,"Listen, what I thought seems to be true now, as long as it's going on." Rajesh said curiously,"I mean? Did Rafiq meet you?"" Rudra said very seriously,"Yes, and from what I heard from him and from what I understood that there is a conspiracy going on here, behind everything."

"What's going on?" Rajesh asked,

"He said that too, but I didn't understand, he said, everyone here is like an animal, and everyone is making millions by selling it."

" I mean?"Rajesh asked in amazement.

"I don't know what happened to me before I realized it, and I'm here when I open my eyes."

After a while, in a heavy voice, Rudra looked around and saw Nigam coming. He entered and said,"How are you now?"

Trying to sit up straight, Rudra said,"Better, but the head is too heavy."

Nigam said very seriously,"You are sick, so I am silent, Mr. Rudra, but what you have done is not right."

Rudra said,"If some people fall prey to Shekhar tomorrow to protect your rules, would it be very good?"

"But you weren't at Shekhar's cell? You were expected to be taken from another cell."

Rudra said,"Everyone works in his own way, Mr. Nigam."

Nigam looked at Rudra for a moment and said,"Get well soon, Mr. Rudra, we'll talk later."

Rudra watched Nigam leave, then said to Rajesh,"Slowly they too are realizing that some truth, which they want to convey to the people, is coming to light."

Rajesh told Rudra that he has a useful job, he is coming again in the evening, so Rajesh left. Rudra slowly closed his eyes and tried to rest, but could not understand when he fell asleep. Suddenly Rudra felt as if his lips were tied to someone else's wet lips Rudra's eyes opened, she removed his lips and asked"How are you, Rudra?"

Rudra was a little shocked to see Shelley in the hospital like this, asked"Are you here?"

"No, I couldn't come, I couldn't help but look at the hand that introduced me to my body and mind."

Today, Shelley's eyes seem to be talking about something else, with a mysterious look telling her, forget it, it's a hospital, you're sick, satisfy me. Shelley slowly started kissing Rudra's neck like crazy. Suddenly he left Rudra and stood up Rudra looked at Shelley a little surprised. Shelley straightened her clothes and said"I have to go; Dr. Kapoor is coming" and somehow ran out of the room. And after a while, Kapoor came and stood Rudra was even more surprised to see Kapoor, not understanding how Shelley understood that Dr. Kapoor was coming.

Kapoor said,"Do you know the problem with you, your situation is like naughty school children, have you given a little concession, will do something that will bring the trouble of the world on your shoulders"

Rudra asked"I don't understand"

"I told you to stay out for a while that day, I didn't tell you to go to Unit B and cause trouble", then after a while he pulled Rudra's eye and said"Leave, how are you feeling now"

Rudra said,"Everything is fine, but the head is impossibly heavy."

Kapoor said,"It doesn't matter. I'm on medication."

Rudra said"OK"

Kapoor said in a kind tone of request"Please, as long as you are here, my responsibility is you, stay a little right, then get out of now and go where you want to go."

Rudra laughed and said,"I promise, but how long I can keep that depends on how long you keep me here."

"Then, I promise, I won't go anywhere," replied Rudra with a laugh

Talking to Rudra, Kapoor explained a medicine to the nurse and left. The nurse fed Rudra with medicine and water, then fixed the pillow on his head and laid him down. He said,"Try to sleep a little, you will see everything will be fine."

Rudra lay down slowly, then slowly fell asleep in his eyes, but he did not understand.

14

Rudra was released from the hospital exactly two days later. This time he must go to the jungle, no matter what and no matter what, Shekhar must be found. Rudra came to his room and saw that he still kept his watch, phone and even the pen as it was. Rudra came back to his room and sat on his bed, then called Raju and asked him to bring a cup of tea. Rudra had just started thinking about Rajesh, Rajesh came into the room. Rudra looked at Rajesh and said"I was thinking about you, will you have tea? Then call Raju once and tell him", Rajesh shook his head and said that he will not drink tea anymore, he has just eaten. Rajesh said"How are you feeling now, are you healthy?"

" Yes, a lot" he said, leaning his body back on the bed"Even if I am not healthy, I must be healthy, still in the Shekhar forest, he must be found."

"How?" Rajesh asked.

"I'll go out today, after this tea." Then he looked at Rajesh and said,"Are you coming with me?"

Raju came with tea and appeared before them for a while. After having tea, Rudra and Rajesh went out on the way to the forest. As soon as they did not go far, they entered the forest. Gradually they go deeper and deeper into the jungle, the weather is good enough today, the sun is helping with its radiant rays. As the sun shines through the gaps in the trees, it has turned the forest into a dander today, as if a bird is greeting them from behind, and saying, you are our guests, be careful to cross the forest. You are not afraid of any beast in this forest, if you are afraid of a man of flesh and blood like you, who may be waiting for you somewhere in this forest to prey on you. After reaching some distance, Rudra stood up, seeing Rudra, Rajesh also stood up, Rajesh asked,"What's the matter, sir?"

Rudra was silent for a while and said"there is no point in going to one side at a time, you look to the right, I am going to the left"

Rajesh said in a slightly offensive tone,"But where is Shekhar, we don't know. If we separate, the danger may increase."

Rudra said"Did you bring your pistol?"

Rajesh shook his head and said that he had brought it. Rudra took his pistol out of his pocket and said,"If the danger comes true, no one will count the bullets from you."

Rajesh walked to the right of the forest, and Rudra took the pistol in his hand and walked to the left of the forest. Today he feels like a hunter who has gone out to hunt a wild animal in the forest. If the leaves of a light tree move, it seems as if Shekhar is watching from behind, who knows, maybe he is really watching. Rudra sent Rajesh under the influence of his obduracy, now he is beginning to think, if there is any real danger to Rajesh. Rudra's acquaintance with him is why he seems to be close to Rajesh Rudra has lived a life like this ever since his wife and daughter died, this is the first time he wants to think of someone as a friend, he is worried about someone. Rudra has come a long way from these thoughts, his surprise was suddenly broken by the sound of a foot coming from a nearby bush. It seems that the bush moved a little? Rudra walked towards the bush with the pistol in his hand. As soon as he removed the bush, he saw someone running in the opposite direction with a sigh. His face was not very clear, he could see him from behind. Rudra follows the shadow without thinking of anything else. He runs along the winding forest path, noticing the shadows, somewhere high, somewhere low. The shadow seemed to disappear after a long run. Rudra gasps. When he looked around, he began to think that Rudra had come to this place before. Going a little further, he noticed the broken church where he had taken refuge with Rajesh on the day of the disaster. Rudra could not understand, then the shadow has entered here?

With that in mind, he grabbed his pistol and walked slowly toward the church door. The door was ajar, so with a little push the huge door opened Rudra entered the church very slowly with gingerly. At the sound of the door, some pigeons inside the church became frightened and flew randomly. Looking back and forth, Rudra entered the church a little further. Suddenly someone pushed him hard from behind, Rudra fell face down, the pistol dropped from his hand and went away. Rudra tried to look around while lying on the ground. As he lay on the ground, he saw that he looked a lot like him, with two bloodshot eyes staring at him through the gap in his hair lying in front of his face. This time he sat on his knees in front of Rudra and said"Hello, Mr. Rudra, how are you?"

Rudra asked in surprise"Do you know me?"

He smiled lightly and said,"Why don't I recognize you? You're looking for me, and I don't know you?"

Rudra said"Shekhar?"

"Yes, I am Shekhar, you have been sent here to find me" Then Shekhar himself stood up straight, then extended his hand towards Rudra. Rudra took his hand and stood up. Then he said,"You can't run away unjustly for long, Shekhar."

Shekhar laughed, then said,"First of all, I did not run away unjustly, and secondly, you did not find me, but I found you."

"Even if you hadn't found me, I would have found you,"

Shekhar laughed like crazy, then said,"Have you had the habit of daydreaming since you were little?"

"I don't understand the meaning" Rudra asked frowning

"This is the rule Rudra Sen, whoever you look for, he is looking for you" Shekhar replied with a smile

"Who are you looking for, Shekhar, you are running away, you have come to this hospital after killing your wife and child for your own psychiatric treatment, you have also run away from there, with what hope?" Rudra asked

Shekhar laughed and said,"You have seen what has been shown to you, Rudra Sen. I did not kill my wife and children, they fabricated a case against me, I killed two Pakistani extremists who tried to kill my family. Big game of politics Rudra Sen, you're still a kid to them." Shekhar walked silently for a while towards the pistol lying on the ground of Rudra, then picked up the pistol from the ground and handed it to Rudra and said"Shekhar cannot be killed with these toys."

Surprised, Rudra took the pistol from Shekhar, then Shekhar said,"The court declared me a mental patient and sent me here for treatment."

Rudra put the pistol in the back of his pants and said"But why did you run away?"

Shekhar said:"World War II began in 1939, when a group of German scientists conducted a study to find out what kind of chemical reaction the human brain would become like a robot, and the way you run it would work. Germany wanted this process to be based on the Soviet Union That's what they're doing here, they're doing that research on all the patients, and a lot of people have died as a result I know they wanted to kill me, but I escaped."

"Everything is slowly getting clearer in front of me now. Despite having 80 patients in my record, I have personally investigated 67 patients, I don't understand where the other 13 have gone."

Shekhar sat down in a chair in the church and said,"Now if you understand everything."

"Yeah, but I don't understand a thing. Why are you hiding in the woods?"

Rudra asked Shekhar with a smile and replied"How can you cross the river, there are sing and guards," then he got up from his chair and said"But I will escape, I want to see the end of the Murthy and the Nigam once."

Rudra pulled out a pistol and said,"Maybe you're right, what happened to you wasn't right, but I have to finish the job I'm here for, now raise your hand and come with me."

Shekhar laughed again and said,"How can you do DIA work with so few memories, Rudra? I said, Shekhar can't be killed or caught with this toy."

Shekhar said there was a big cloth inside the church, maybe something had been pressed with it for many years, he picked it up with one hand and threw it at Rudra. It was getting dark in the dust all around, Rudra covered his eyes with both hands, with a sudden push Rudra ran out through the door. Rudra somehow ran after Shekhar and came out of the church.

He came and saw Rajesh standing, he was coming here looking for Rudra.

Rudra quickly said"Can't you catch him?"

Rajesh was surprised and said"Who will I catch?"

Rudra said"Shekhar, ran away, didn't you see him run away?" Rajesh was equally surprised and replied"Where, no?" Rudra was surprised, did not understand how Shekhar escaped, and did not see Rajesh? Did it go out of the church and merge into the air?

15.

Rajesh and Rudra came walking through the forest and appeared on the bank of the river There was a look of remorse in Rudra's eyes, but he ran away At the same time, thousands of questions were running through my mind, such a big conspiracy, where people use people like guinea pigs. They once swore to serve the country and the people, today they are making people their victims for power and money. Maybe Shekhar is guilty of this, but they are more guilty than that Besides, Shekhar said that if what happened to him is true, then he has been framed Was Shekhar really mentally deranged, or was he hanged and used here for research? Rudra was thinking these things with one mind. Rudra came across the river and noticed that it was not the place where they came from, it was the other side of the river. Looking around,

Rudra said,"We didn't come this way, it's the other side."

Rajesh looked around and said"I understand that, but which way did I come?"

Rudra looked around, then took a cigarette out of his pocket, lit it and sat down under a tree, then said,"How did that escape?"

Rajesh was very surprised and asked"I still do not understand, Shekhar met you? And you say he ran away in front of me, while I was out then, where, I did not see anyone?"

"I wonder, did it get out of the church?"

Rajesh slowly came and sat next to Rudra, then said"What happened in the forest?"

Rudra began to say,"He was looking at me from a bush. I saw him and chased him. He went into the old church. I followed him into the church. I did not understand. He suddenly pushed me from behind. I stumbled and my pistol fell out of my hand."

Rajesh asks with great curiosity"Then, what happened?"

"Surprisingly, he called my name and said he knew me. What a strange thing. He grabbed me and I was shocked by what he heard."

"What did he say?"

"He said he killed, but not his family. He killed two extremists, then he was trapped and brought here."

"But why did he run away?"

"Patients' brains are being studied here, and a lot of patients have died in doing so," he said to Rajesh in silence for a while, then Said"Now you understand, even though we have eighty patients in our record, we got some sixty-seven, we didn't get any of the remaining thirteen?"

Rajesh said in surprise,"I can't believe it, but they need to be handcuffed so that it doesn't happen to anyone else in the future. It's completely illegal."

Rudra smiled lightly and said,"Those who talk about making rules are the real conspirators here. A huge circle, where you have to bring their real character to the world's attention, but be careful, don't be arrogant."

Rajesh asked"So, is Shekhar mentally healthy?"

Rudra said"I understand that, Shekhar is much healthier than those who are running this cycle here"

Rajesh said"But sir, Shekhar had a full chance to kill you, but did not kill, why? For what?"

Rudra thought for a moment and said seriously,"He knew why I was here, and who I am. He knew I would be here one day, and he was waiting for me so he could tell me all about them." Then he got up, walked a little towards the river and said"but he escaped"

Rajesh said"What should we do now?"

"Shekhar will come forward only when Murti and Nigam are punished, and he will not leave here until they are punished."

Rajesh said very worriedly"But how?"

Rudra replied,"We have to find out first, where is this research, I mean, where is the laboratory? Once I find it, I can pull off their masks."

Rajesh said that this time they need to go back, because the evening is coming down, they have to go back through the jungle road, there is a possibility of getting lost, so now they need to go back. Rudra and Rajesh return through the forest. After all the work is done, all the birds are coming back to their homes, the fear of death that engulfed them when they came, why that fear is no more. Shekhar doesn't seem to be that scary anymore, it's as if there is a magic for him, it seems that someone has put him in a lot of danger, and Shekhar is wandering helplessly in this forest, he needs help. Slowly darkness descended into the forest. They are running fast to get out of the jungle Rudra wondered why he had come here, and slowly came to know how much he was involved in the magic of a strange mystery. There is a terrible conspiracy going on, where some educated animals are playing with people's brains, who will hunt them? Rudra and Rajesh came to their bungalow.

Rajesh said to Rudra"Sir, today is a very strange day"

'The day is not strange, but it is an experience, what you see or what you know is not true, there is a mystical reality behind it which is different from your imagination," Rudra replied very seriously.

16.

Rudra was called to the Nigam's office in the early hours of the morning. Rudra and Rajesh came and appeared in the office of the Nigam. Seeing Rudra, Nigam came forward and asked him to sit down, then went out on his own for a while. After a while, he came back with Dr. Kapoor. Then he looked at Rajesh and asked him to go out, because both Nigam and Dr. Kapoor wanted to talk to Rudra in private. Rajesh looked at Rudra once and then walked out Nigam closed the door of his room and came back. Rudra did not understand what they wanted, Nigam took a file from Kapoor and said"Mr. Rudra, do you know what is in this file?"

Rudra said in astonishment,"Tell me, I don't understand."

Nigam looked at Kapoor and said to him,"Doctor Kapoor, it would be good if you said a little tidy."

Kapoor said,"Of course." He looked at Rudra and said"When you were in the hospital bed, we did some tests on you, including your headaches, and with it getting sick again and again, we did some tests on your brain,"

Rudra asked in surprise."What did you get in that test?"

"We've got a spot in your brain that indicates LBD. Don't worry, it's nothing. You'll get well."

Rudra sat quietly for a while, then said,"What do you mean?"

"Suppose at first there is a headache, insomnia, dizziness, these are the first, but if not treated in time, it gradually turns into hallucinations or split personality." Kapoor tried to convince him.

Rudra asked seriously,"Shekhar had this problem, didn't he? You said Dr. Kapoor."

Kapoor tried to convince Rudra,"Yes, but it was terrible, yours will get better."

Nigam put his hand on Rudra's shoulder and said,"Please, don't be upset, you are in the middle of us, so we will do our best to heal you."

Rudra said,"Once this case is settled, I will go back to Calcutta. I will go there for treatment."

Nigam said,"Surely you will do what you think, but as long as you are here, it is our responsibility to take care of you."

Without further ado, Rudra asked,"What is my next step? What do I have to do?"

Kapoor said"You come to the unit tomorrow morning, I will stay"

Rudra agreed that he would go to the unit the next day to meet Kapoor, and then left. As soon as he came out of the Nigam's office, he saw Rajesh Singh standing and talking Seeing Rudra, Singh said"Is it a meeting?"

Rudra smiled somehow and said"Yes, what else"

"Did you get any news about Shekhar?"

"No, but I'll get it."

"Look, who is the dangerous patient who should be shot as soon as he tries?"

"means?"

"Look, Mr. Rudra, from a tiger wounded in the forest to a mad dog on the road, two speed guns," said Singh with a smile.

Rudra took a cigarette out of his pocket and lit it. Then he looked at Singh and said,"Sometimes a lot of things come up when you go looking for something scary, which may not be a good thing for many, so it's better to come up with some unknown secrets slowly."

Singh smiled softly and said goodbye. Seeing Rudra's worried face, Rajesh asked,"Is everything all right?"

Rudra said equally seriously,"Let's go somewhere else, we can't talk here."

With Rudra Rajesh, he chose a place surrounded by a garden a little further away to speak for himself. Some women were working in the garden, looking at them as if they had come to a different planet, and instead of welcoming them, they looked at them in amazement and wondered, what do you want to do here?

Rudra came and sat on a chair in the garden, Rajesh came and sat next to him and asked"Now tell me, sir, what happened? You are feeling restless."

Rudra was a little worried and said in a slightly upset voice,"Kapoor said, when I was sick, they tested me, and they got LBD symptoms in me."

Surprised Rajesh said,"Shekhar had this problem, didn't he?"

"Yeah, that's what I'm wondering, is that my problem so Shekhar?" Rudra said looking at Rajesh in amazement

"So, what did you say" Rajesh asked

"I said, I will go to Calcutta for treatment after settling everything here"

"But what is the reason for doing this?"

"The reason is very clear Rajesh, they have understood that I will leak their curtain when, so they want to remove me" Rudra said

Rajesh said"It is not possible, the Nigam will have to answer to the higher authority, if anything happens to us"

"Yeah, if anything, you'll tell me that Shekhar was killed in the woods, if you understand," he said after thinking for a while,"or maybe it's, my brain is the next what they are looking for."

Rajesh became a little upset, Rajesh got up, went a little further, lit a cigarette, gave another to Rudra, then said,"If that happens, we have very little time, and we have to get out of here as soon as we can."

Rudra let out a puff of smoke and said,"Unfortunately, it's not as straightforward as you say, friend."

"What are you thinking of doing then?" Rudra also got up and stood beside Rajesh, then said,"Think about it, there is no other way."

"What are you thinking of doing then?"

"As Shekhar must be caught, so must their truth be brought to the fore." Rudra also got up and stood beside Rajesh, then said,"Think about it, there is no other way."

Rajesh said"but I don't understand why you are taking such a big risk, it is our job to catch Shekhar, we will see the next one"

Rudra smiled and said"Do you think I can get out so easily from now on? Never. The reason I woke up after three days was because they kept me awake, because that's when they gave me brain tests and whatever medicine they gave me."

Then he turned his face and looked at Unit A and said,"Now call me in cant and tell me, get ready, your name and the other thirteen are written."

Rajesh said,"But anyway, we have to get out from now on."

Then he said to Rajesh,"I am not afraid to die, and I have no reason to live today, but I will put an end to this injustice."

Today, for the first time, Rajesh saw a new look in Rudra, as if he was a real soldier who never hesitates to give his life for the country, no matter where the enemy is, inside or outside the country.

17.

There is an explanation for a deep sleep and drowsiness at night, which perhaps no one understands better than Rudra. As the night deepens, a storm of questions surrounds him, who, why, why or how the biggest question. The habit of sleeping with the door of the house closed from the beginning, today and there was nothing wrong with him, but hearing a strange sound, Rudra looked around the door from the bed. The door is slowly opening The light from the garden outside came out of his house As soon as the door was slightly open, he came to his room and reached inside his room Surprised, he looked at the door and wondered if the door had opened, or if he had forgotten to close it. Suddenly Rudra noticed that a shadow of someone had come outside and followed the path of light inside his room. Rudra looked at the door more surprised, then asked"Who is there?"

This time the door opened a little more, he saw Rudra, the shadow covered from head to toe and stood in front of his bed. Rudra tried to sit up but could not, as if someone had taken all his strength, the force of sitting up with his own hands was also unable Rudra, as if an inertia had swallowed his nerves. Slowly the shadow came in front of him and sat beside him on the bed, removing the veil from his head, asking"How are you now?"

This time there was no more shadow, his face was clearly clear even in that darkness, there was a light of darkness in his words, in that light Rudra looked at him with some surprise and some fear and said"Who are you?"

Strangely awkward and horrible that face, one side of the face burning in the fire, the eyes are almost hanging out, the lips are nothing, the teeth inside the mouth came out in the form of a skeleton, she laughed and said"You don't recognize? That beautiful afternoon we spent, you forgot. You're the man in my life who reconciled my body and mind. I haven't forgotten. That's what happened that day. What do you do if you forget?"

Rudra realized that his throat was trembling, he could feel the throbbing of his heart, as if he would be stunned this time. Rudra asked in a frightened voice,"Shelley, are you?"

Shelley laughed and replied,"If you recognize me,"

"What's the matter with you?"

"He shot and killed me, then burned me. I've seen the funeral of my dreams and aspirations. My love, tell me how can I go without seeing you once before I say goodbye forever?"

Rudra realized that the sweat from his head was slowly touching his eyebrows and falling on his eyelids, his vision was getting blurred, Rudra said"I mean, you are dead? Who killed you?"

Shelley laughed and said,"It's a very strange question."

Suddenly another woman's voice came to Rudra's ears. When she entered the room, he didn't understand,the woman's voice said,"he's like this all the time,he can't remember anything, andhe asks questions when asked."

Rudra looked at him in amazement, his wife was standing there, Rudra was surprised and said"Are you here?"

"I told you, I'm with you wherever you are, I'm always by your side."

Rudra once looked at his wife and once at Shelley and said"I don't understand anything, you ...?"

It didn't end there, a strange smile from the two of them on him, as if creating panic in the whole house. Rudra couldn't take it anymore, he felt as if his ears were bursting and blood was coming out, Rudra woke up.What kind of dream was this? What a terrible dream, he could not understand anything. Rudra drank from a glass of water on the table next to his bed, then came out and stood on the balcony.It's like a sultry environment, no more air today, as if nature is signaling something bad to happen. Rudra's mind did not rest on the balcony, he slowly went down to the garden and sat on a bench. It's as if there's a lot of discomfort all over his body, and he was out of breath. Are any of these dreams coming? Is it the effect of a medicine in the hospital? What a thumping environment, all can hear is the call of the beetle and sometimes a patch somewhere. Suddenly someone said from the side,"Didn't you sleep today?"

Rudra looked around in surprise and saw the old woman sitting next to him Rudra looked at him and said"Oh, you? Don't you sleep at night too?"

The woman laughed and said,"Sleep. Do you think we're all awake? The fact is, we're all asleep. Just want a man to wake up. I'm trying to do that."

"Tell me today, who are you? Where do you live?" Rudra asked

The woman laughed again."Why do you ask the same question over and over again? Someone has come to see you, look at that." The woman pointed her finger in front of him.

Rudra stood up and looked at Shekhar, then said"You are here, if you come by yourself for surrender."

Shekhar smiled, then said,"No one can catch me, and you never can."

"What do you mean, why can't I catch you when you've come here, and I won't let you go now?" Rudra said excitedly.

"You are dreaming falsely, and the biggest thing is, you stepped on the way I warned you about, you're stuck, you're stuck, will you catch me? Will you be able to save yourself?"

Rudra said"I will understand that, but now you have to go with me"

Shekhar did not smile this time, came to Rudra and said"I know where their laboratory, I am not an enemy, I just want to save the rest of the patients, help me Rudra"

Rudra did not listen to Shekhar and said,"I will unmask them, but I have to complete the work for which I have come here, and that is to find you and hand over you to them."

Shekhar looked at Rudra for a while, then said,"Okay, you unmask them, I promise, I'll come with you and surrender myself, because you can't find them without my help."

Then Shekhar stood in front of Rudra and put his hand on his shoulder and said"Our job is to protect this country and country people, let's go together, friend, let's destroy these enemies inside the country together. I promise, then I will surrender to you, because you will catch me. That's the decent thing to do, and it should end there."

Rudra said,"Where is their laboratory?"

"There is a house by the river, surrounded by dense forest, there," said Shekhar.

Rudra agreed with Shekhar, then said,"Okay, so be it, I will accept you as my friend and I will destroy them with you, but then you will surrender to me, or I will be forced to force you."

Shekhar smiled and said"I agree"

Then Rudra looked at the woman again, asked Shekhar"Do you know her? Do you know who she is?"

Shekhar smiled and walked over to the woman, then put his right hand on her shoulder and said very affectionately "oh Rudra, you don't recognize her? She is my mother."

Rudra realized that the call of the bird was slowly reaching his ears, the light of dawn was slowly being prepared to touch the nature, the night passed and dawn came almost. Maybe this time everyone will get a new morning, a new morning, the beginning of a new day, a new hope.

18.

A trap of death, in which Rudra seems to be slowly becoming a prisoner People are one way and another way Today he has found Shekhar, but he does not seem to be a criminal today The judgment that was given to him as a mental patient, now Rudra feels that the judgment should have been given to the people here who are playing with people's lives in the name of treatment. A lot of time has been wasted, if a little effort had been made, maybe Shelley could have been saved. But Shelley was really dead, but that's what happened, that was dreamed. These words keep revolving in Rudra's head all the time. Rudra left without wasting time and went to Kapoor's bungalow, Rudra reaches after going some distance. The doorbell rang, but no one answered. After playing many times, he noticed that the door was locked from outside, so there was no one Rudra kept thinking, if such a big accident had really happened, the crowd would have gathered here by now, and these news would not have been suppressed, he would have known exactly.

Rudra did not meet Shelley, after a while he came back to his bungalow When he came back, he saw Rajesh standing on the balcony in front of Rudra's house Seeing Rudra, Rajesh came down with a gnashing of teeth, came and asked Rudra"Where have you been? Has he called you many times?"

Rudra asked very seriously"Who?"

"Doctor Kapoor, you had an appointment this morning, he was waiting for you" Rajesh replied very busy.

"No, I don't need treatment, it's their requirements" He sat on the bench and said,"I've got the laboratory."

Rajesh is very excited and says"Where is it?"

"By the river, inside an old house surrounded by forest, all this research is done there. I am going now, let's go with me" Rudra said

"definitely I am with you, but where did you get this news from?"

Rudra looked at Rajesh for a while and said,"When oppression and injustice become excessive, then the way to end it is ready. Look at the history." Then he looked around for a while in silence, then said"listen carefully, some invisible helpless people, like us, who at one time swore to save the country, are asking for help and revenge.

I don't have much time in my hands. I have to finish the work soon. Let's go."

Rajesh heard all about Rudra, then said"Then what will you say to Murthy, Nigam and Kapoor?"

Rudra said,"There is nothing more to say or hear, my friend. Come on, it's time to do something. The memory of the darkness that covers the human mind is a lot like acceptance, but after that acceptance comes a change, and it's time to witness that change.""It's not too late, friend. Let's go."

Rudra went out to the forest with Rajesh. They walked through the jungle to the river, Rudra is looking around again and again, as if looking for someone. Rajesh noticed that and asked"Are you looking for someone?"

Rudra said"Yes, Shekhar will come, to show me the way"

Rajesh was surprised and said"What are you talking about, I don't understand anything, where did he meet you?"

Rudra said"He came to our bungalow last night to meet me"

"And you let him go? It would have been over"Rajesh said very excitedly

"Don't worry, Shekhar will surrender" Rudra smiled and relaxed to Rajesh. They came to the river to see Rajesh As soon as Rudra came to the bank of the river, he started running from side to side, then after a while he said,"Shekhar said, if you go a little further to the left, the house is next to the river surrounded by forest." Saying that, Rudra ran to the left.

Rajesh stood speechless for a while, he didn't really understand anything After five minutes, Rudra came back panting, with a satisfied smile on his face Rajesh is still speechless, looking at Rudra with a dumb look Rudra looked at him and smiled and said,"You don't have to look surprised anymore. Shekhar is right, I have got the laboratory."

Rajesh got very excited and said,"Let's go inside and finish their game today."

Rudra stood up, took a cigarette out of his pocket and lit it, then said,"Let's go, but wait a minute."

Rudra said,"Shekhar is supposed to come here, he will guide the rest." A reassuring impression on Rudra today, then he said to Rajesh,"I will unmask them today, and I will take Shekhar to the right place so that he can be treated properly."

After a while, Rudra told Rajesh to wait by the river and ran back to the forest, telling Rajesh that he was bringing Shekhar very soon. Rudra starts looking for Shekhar in the forest. As if the scent of liberation spreads all around today, death will return back today, the rhythm of life will be renewed, a strange stream of joy and excitement starts flowing from inside Rudra. Rudra came looking for

Shekhar and came back to the broken church Rudra stood in front of the church and looked at the church door, saw the church door open and Shekhar coming out. Shekhar smiled and stood up to Rudra and said,"Then did you find the laboratory?"

Rudra sighed and said,"Yes, I got it, let's go, show me the rest of the road, I'll finish all their games today."

Shekhar said,"I knew you could, friend. You go ahead."

Rudra was surprised and said"You are not coming?"

Shekhar said"Who said I am not coming, I am coming with you, you reach, I am coming after you, as your shadow"

Rudra said,"Okay, come on, I'm waiting by the river. I've actually left a friend of mine standing there." he said, he would wait for Shekhar.

Rudra came running again and appeared by the river. Rudra was surprised when he came to the river, Rajesh is not there. Rudra was surprised, he told Rajesh to stand here. Rudra started calling Rajesh's name, Rudra's voice echoed around and came back to him, but Rajesh did not come back. Rudra keeps looking here and there. Suddenly, a little farther down the slope of the river after looking at Rudra. Rudra runs and reaches there, the same, whose body is here after? Rudra quickly came down the slope of the river, Rudra was shocked to see the body lying on his back, the same Rajesh Wet in blood near the chest, who killed him? A strange suppressed cry came out of Rudra's chest.

After losing everything, it was as if he thought of Rajesh as a close friend. Leaving the body down, Rudra came up again on the slop, then started running backwards again. After going quiet, a bit, it was as if there was a collision with someone Rudra stood up and saw with tears in his eyes that he had collided with Shekhar.

Shekhar said to Rudra"What happened?"

Rudra said,"They killed my friend. I told him to wait here. I went to see you. Come back and see his body."

Shekhar wanted to know where Rajesh's body was. Rudra brings him to the slope of the river where Rajesh's body is lying Rudra shows his finger, but Shekhar is surprised and asks Rudra about the dead body again, because there was no body. Rudra sees the place well now, he is not only surprised not to find Rajesh's body, he is also very upset, he continues to explain to Shekhar that he had seen his body here a while ago, covered in blood.

Shekhar puts his hand on Rudra's shoulder and says,"I agree with you, my friend, and it is also known that your friend has been killed, and where is his body now?"

Rudra can't say anything to Shekhar, just looks at him with a questioninglook.Shekhar shows the broken house, which has hidden itself in the jungle, and is intoxicated with death by the river.

19

Sadness, anger or grievances, Rudra lost the state of mind to understand who to tell. He understood today that human life is based on work and relationships. Whatever the reason for his coming here to complete the task, today's reason is pulling him for the task, he needs a lot more. Rudra is realizing at every moment how great it is to have a friend in a lonely life, losing Rajesh. Rudra, out of anger and grief, took his pistol out of his pocket and started running towards the laboratory with a sigh. After a while, he suddenly found a white car in front of him. Rudra noticed Singh standing guard in front of the laboratory door, with two others. Rudra realized that it was very difficult to get inside with a pistol. Rudra went and stood behind a tree, then looked around once.

Somehow Rudra came to the car without anyone noticing Then he took the handkerchief out of his pocket He then opened the lid of the petrol tanker in front of the car, inserted the handkerchief and soaked it in oil. Then he put the handkerchief in the tank and hung the rest of it outside. He lit a fire in it and ran away hiding behind another tree. The fire grabbed the handkerchief and slowly moved towards the tank of the car, but Rudra was startled. His wife is standing in front of the car and his daughter is holding her hand, looking at him with a helpless look. There is no fear in their eyes, there is no sorrow, only one hope, the hope of getting everything back, Rudra's wife was looking at him, and tears were coming down her eyes.

Rudra looked at the car behind them, and it was not too late, the fire would reach its destination this time, he waved his hand and motioned for them to move, repeatedly telling them to move, but they stood still. Suddenly there was a huge explosion, a fireplace that swallowed everything. Rudra's eyes were helpless, tears, he saw his wife and daughter swallowed up in the fire. But strangely enough, he saw the fire and the black smoke disappear as if they were still standing there. Then they walked slowly to the other side.

Rudra regained his composure, then saw the sound of the explosion and the fire, and Singh and his two companions came running towards him. Rudra saw that they were busy putting out the fire, then Rudra entered the house without anyone noticing. As soon as he entered, he saw a wooden staircase going up, Rudra kept going up the stairs, sometimes some doors were falling, but Rudra noticed that all the doors were locked. One by one he climbed the stairs and reached the last door, the door half open and half close. Rudra took the pistol out of his pocket, then grabbed the device with both hands and came very slowly to the door. Then he closed his eyes for a while, as if he opened his eyes again with some courage and some vengeance, then he suddenly opened the door and went inside and raised the pistol.

A huge house, almost completely empty Just in the middle of the room is a big table and chair, and in that chair sits Mr. Rajagopalan Murthy. Seeing Rudra, Murthy said,"We have finally met." Murthy looked at Rudra, then picked up the receiver of the phone on the table and said,"He's here."

Rudra slowly put the pistol towards the idol and came forward and said"My friend came with me here, where is he?"

Murthy laughed and said,"Since when have you been so friendly, Lieutenant Shekhar Chopra?"

Rudra was surprised and asked,"Who is Shekhar Chopra? I am DIA agent Rudra Sen."

Murthy laughed and replied,"That's the name we gave you, you were in our treatment, you are. You ran away from now, and you were brought back here, and the responsibility was given to the DIA."

Rudra laughs and replies"Wrong Mr. Murthy, the way you want to trap me here, I will never let that happen, because I understood all your games long ago. And most importantly, Shekhar is with me, I have found him."

Murthy came forward towards Rudra's open pistol and said,"Where is Shekhar, you have entered this room alone."

Rudra did not notice for so long that Shekhar was not with him, Rudra did not drop his pistol, he kept saying"I will bring Shekhar and prove everything, and also prove that you are playing a death game with the sick people here."

After a while, Dr. Kapoor opened the door and entered Seeing the open pistol in Rudra's hand, Dr. Kapoor was a little surprised and said"What happened here?" Then he looked at Rudra and said"What's the matter Shekhar, where did you go?" Rudra shouted"I am not Shekhar, I am Rudra Sen, you are repeatedly trying to prove me Shekhar, I know why."

Murthy said,"It is our job to prove Shekhar to Shekhar."

Rudra began to say,"Here you are doing research on the brains of the patients. Eighty patients in the record you sent and sixty-seven here, do you have any of the remaining thirteen? Despite not having Shekhar, there are sixty-seven people as a mill, less than one, why? You said Rafiq is not here, but I met Rafiq myself, he admitted that he killed my family himself. And the biggest reason Shekhar came here is that he has been framed, Shekhar fled to save himself, today he wants to save the rest, so that it does not happen to them. So, your face needs to come out in front of everyone."

Kapoor once looked at the Murthy, then asked Rudra,"Who told you these things?"

Rudra was very excited, but he smiled and said,"When the oppression increases, people are ready to help those who come forward to get rid of that oppression."

Kapoor said"But Shekhar, you understand one thing .."

Rudra didn't let him finish talking, he got very excited and ran to Kapoor, then he put the pistol on his head and said"I am not Shekhar, I am Rudra" then he lowered the pistol and said"I won't let any of you go, you killed my friend too, and hid his body."Then he said to Kapoor again," You ask Shelley, who am I? Or have you driven her crazy for so long?"

Kapoor was trying to say something again, Murthy stopped him by showing his hand, then asked Rudra"Who is Shelley?"

Rudra smiled a little frogly and said,"Why, Mr. Murthy, you don't know Dr. Kapoor's wife."

This time Kapoor laughed and came to Rudra and said,"Five years ago today, my wife died in cancer. I couldn't save her even if I became a doctor myself."

Rudra shouted,"Wrong, you got married five years ago today, and Shelley was unhappy with you for leading an unjust life."

Murthy began to say,"Dr. Kapoor is our best doctor here. His wife died five years ago. It's true." He pointed to the door and said,"Look over there, you were probably looking for him."

Rudra looked back, and was surprised to see Rajesh has come and stood in the room, and there is no question in his eyes today, no hesitation in anything, very naturally he said to Rudra"What happened, any difficulty?"

20.

Rudra was surprised to see Rajesh, but at the same time he felt happy, he ran to Rajesh, touched him well, then said"I thought maybe I lost you forever, you are not just my assistant today, you are my best friend."Rudra looked at everyone once, then said to Rajesh"Look what they are saying, I came here with you, didn't I?" Rajesh said very easily"I don't understand what the problem is"

Rudra said to Rajesh"They forgot who I am, you remind them."

Rajesh smiled and said"You are Lieutenant Shekhar Chopra"

Rudra looked at Rajesh in surprise, then said"If I am Shekhar, who are you?"

"I am DIA agent Rajesh Sharma" Rajesh said in serious note

Rudra got up and shouted seriously, then ran towards Rajesh"Unfaithful, did you cheat on me?"

Then he picked up the pistol in his hand and fired at Murthy, then Rajesh hurriedly took out his pistol, Rudra turned the pistol on him and shot Rajesh. Rudra saw Murthy and Rajesh standing in their own place, nothing happened to them. Rudra stared at his pistol in disbelief.

Rudra turned his pistol to look at his cartridge, his pistol smashed in the middle like a clay toy. Rudra stared in amazement, then looked at everyone once in amazement. Everyone in the house seemed to be looking at Rudra with a look of sympathy Murthy came forward and said,"If all else fails, I would like to show you something."

Saying this, he took out a file from the table and showed it to Rudra. When Rudra opened the file, the first thing he saw was a picture of him, his name written on the side was Shekhar Chopra, and the reason for the punishment was killing his own family, and details of his treatment in subsequent papers. Murthy took the file from Rudra's hand and said,"You were in Cargill, on the battlefield. That's when you had this problem. Rafiq was the cook at your base camp. You've had LBD problems ever since, and the biggest problem with LBD is hallucinosis, as a result, for Rafiq to become a Muslim, you see a Pakistani soldier in him, and shoot him, the defense court proves you are a murderer, and takes you to jail. You were there for about a year, but no one understood your problem, then one day you escaped from prison. In fact, your mental problem made you realize that you are not escaping from an Indian prison, you are escaping from a Pakistani camp. You run away to your house, where your wife and daughter were waiting for you. But when you got there, you spent one day with them, but the next day you had that problem again. Because LBD has two symptoms, one hallucination and two split personalities. You see those Pakistani terrorists in your family too, and shoot them first, then light the gas cylinder and burn the whole house. Then you run away from there, you come back in the evening, but then you forget what you did in the morning before that. You are taken to court again, and it is proved that you have a mental imbalance. Even if you are brought here, run away again because you think someone else has killed your family, to take revenge, because Rajesh got you from your house. You were told another identity, we explained that you are Rudra Sen, and Rajesh brought you here with responsibility, otherwise it was not possible."

Rudra had been listening to everything in silence for so long, this time he said"but Shelley is another ..." Rudra started thinking about all his old memories.

Murthy said"Shelley is your wife's name, look at this" and handed Rudra an identity card and saw Shelley Chopra, his wife.

Rudra slowly sat down on the ground, how dark everything seemed to be to him, then asked,"An old woman often came to see me."

Murthy shows him a picture, Rudra sees it, the picture is a little old, but a young woman, he doesn't recognize it, Rudra says"Who is this? I'm not talking about her, she's too old to come."

Murthy laughed and said,"This is your mother, she died at your birth. You missed your mother from a young age. It was sitting on your head. If your mother were alive today, it would be at this age."

Rudra remembered that night, when he asked Shekhar about the old woman, Shekhar said she was his mother. One by one, Rudra remembers everything, which is a question in itself, to which he will never find an answer. As if a storm was rising across Rudra's chest, he fell to the ground and wanted to cry, but today he is not crying.

Kapoor came forward to Rudra and said, "And your frequent headaches, body aches, were all drug effects."

A groan came out of Rudra in the form of pain, he screamed, a groan, in that scream there was an impossible mental anguish, the pain of losing everything. Rudra finds himself in the form of a dead man, a mental acceptance that has happened in his life, it may end with his life.

Rudra was taken to his cell. Rudra lost consciousness there.

The next morning Rajesh is standing in front of the Nigam's office, now it's time to say goodbye Rajesh was talking outside the officer with a bag in his hand. Singh is waiting in a jeep a short distance away, will take him to the river. Why does Rajesh also seem to be leaving someone here, who is very close, whom the mind does not want to leave. Rajesh has not been able to understand when he has been acting with Rudra for so long as if he has been considered as someone very close to him. If only I could meet you once today.

Murthy shook hands and said,"Thank you very much for your help, and especially your kind help for our medical treatment. What can I say for you?"

Rajesh laughed and said"No no, it's my job, I just did my job just like you, now please allow me then"

Rajesh said goodbye and walked towards the jeep. As soon as he stepped on the jeep, a word came to his ears. Pratima Devi came and said to the Nigam very excitedly"Sir, come quickly, to Shekhar's cell"

Rajesh realized that something had happened, an unknown panic seemed to stir his mind, Rajesh went to Unit B, Shekhar's cell with Murthy and Nigam.

Upon arrival, he saw Dr. Kapoor standing there, a crowd of nurses and ward boys. Rajesh removed everyone and stood in front Rudra alias Shekhar is lying on the ground, sleeping peacefully, his hand is spread out in front, and blood is coming out through the veins of his hand. Rajesh looked at the wall, it was written

"Eclipse is over today,

The new sun will come,

The new dawn will come,

The solution to all the dilemmas today,

I'll be back,

There will be questions ... then?"

The End